The Mystery of the
Shadow Caves

The torch picked out the sheet of black rippling water barring their way, lazily lapping the steps.

'OK,' said Ben. 'That's it.' This was definitely the trap the smugglers had prepared for the Excisemen and he didn't want to hang around any longer. Even Emily stopped and then looked back up the stairs, as if some sixth sense had warned her of impending danger.

A hollow booming sound vibrated down the tunnel, the echo drumming in their ears, a terrible realization creeping over them all.

'What was that?' gasped Emily. But she knew. They all knew. Someone had slid back the rock and, like the Excisemen, they were trapped.

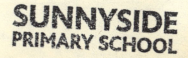

THE MARLOW HOUSE MYSTERIES

1
*The Mystery of
Bloodhound Island*

2
*The Mystery of
the Shadow Caves*

3
*The Mystery of
the White Knuckle Ride*

4
*The Mystery of
Captain Keene's Treasure*

Text copyright © Anthony Masters 1996

First published in Great Britain in 1996
by Macdonald Young Books
61 Western Road
Hove
East Sussex
BN3 1JD

Photoset in North Wales by
Derek Doyle & Associates, Mold, Clwyd.
Printed and bound in Great Britain by
The Guernsey Press Co. Ltd.

British Library Cataloguing in Publication Data available.

ISBN: 0 7500 2159 4
ISBN: 0 7500 2160 8 (pb)

The Marlow House
MYSTERIES
2

THE MYSTERY OF
THE SHADOW CAVES

•

Anthony Masters

'He can't have gone away,' said Alex.

'You said he *never* goes away.' Kate gazed at the signs outside Pearson's Magic Shop and the Roxy Amusement Arcade. They read: CLOSED. GONE ON HOLIDAY. ROY PEARSON.

'Maybe he's done a runner,' speculated Ben. 'Does he owe any money?' He was only half joking. Roy Pearson was well known in Tremaron for permanently living on the edge of bankruptcy.

1

'Of course not,' Alex was indignant. 'He's one of my best mates. OK, he's a lot older than me – but still a mate.' He paused regretfully. 'Roy's new video game machines are amazing. I was going to thrash you.'

'You wouldn't stand a chance against us,' said Kate. 'VRs are in every London arcade. We're professionals.'

'More like addicts,' said Ben and then swiftly returned to the problem. 'So why should Roy go on holiday in June? This is the start of the tourist season. He'll lose a fortune.'

'What about his staff?' Kate was disapproving. 'What are *they* going to do? Sounds as if he might be away for some time if he's done a runner.'

'He hasn't,' insisted Alex. 'Roy would never do a thing like that.'

'Who *does* work for him then?' asked Ben.

'There's old Mrs Cosham in the magic shop. She's a real dragon.'

'That doesn't mean she can afford to be out of work.' Kate was impatient with Alex. He was always moaning if his father's fishing boats had a bad catch. Why couldn't he be more sympathetic to this Mrs Cosham?

'Roy's only got a part-time cashier in the arcade,' Alex continued. 'He used to run that part of the business himself.'

'Well – he's not running it now,' said Kate. The Roxy was one of the few centres of entertainment in Tremaron. The small Cornish town huddled around the harbour, its narrow, winding streets climbing up the hill. The tourists loved the fishing fleet and the little white-washed cottages, but they soon lost interest because there wasn't much to do apart from the arcade and the mini-golf. Even the youth club was shut for the summer.

The town hadn't really changed much in centuries and that was the way the locals wanted it to stay. Most weekends, Ben, Kate and Alex went dinghy sailing and it was wonderful to return to the quiet streets, free from crowds even in summer.

The sour-faced woman was wearing a coat and hat despite the heat, and briskly pushing a shopping trolley.

'Alex Banner,' she began to question him immediately. 'Do *you* know where Roy's gone?'

He shook his head. 'No, Mrs Cosham,' he said with unnatural politeness. He seemed to be afraid of her which was unlike him. Mrs Cosham had obviously got the better of him a long time ago.

Ben eyed her warily. He remembered how

impatient she had been when he had spent ages trying to decide whether to buy stink bombs or itching powder to terrorize Kate. Now Mrs Cosham was looking shocked and afraid beneath her indignation, and Ben was beginning to feel sorry for her.

'I've been down to see the Pearsons but they say he went off last night. Wouldn't tell me when he was coming back. I just can't understand it. Roy *never* goes on holiday.' She stared at Alex suspiciously as if he might have kidnapped him.

'Is he married?' asked Kate curiously. She and Ben had only been in Tremaron for a couple of months and they still hardly knew anyone except for Alex. The town was dominated by fishing families, who were close. Too close, she thought.

'No, although he'd make a lovely dad.' Mrs Cosham's lips thinned. 'He went to lodge with his brother after he fell out with his mum and dad. Got a little niece called Emily. About your age, she is.' She paused, and despite Mrs Cosham's obvious love of gossip, Kate could see that she was upset. 'His brother hasn't seen Roy since he had his tea last night and said he was going away for a while. He didn't say nothing about a holiday when we locked up.' She sniffed disapprovingly. 'Why's he gone off like this then? I'm on my own. Who's going to pay my wages tomorrow if he doesn't show up?' She was close to tears. 'It's not right.'

'Why did he go without telling you?' asked Kate.

'He doesn't owe nothing, if that's what you mean,' Mrs Cosham replied angrily. 'Honest as the day, Roy is. All the wages go out each week, regular as clockwork.' She glared at Kate, as if daring her to disagree.

'His family are on the boats,' said Alex. 'Roy used to be a fisherman. He wouldn't have done anything bad.'

Obviously he and Mrs Cosham would be united in their respect for fishing families and Roy Pearson's good record, thought Ben. They wouldn't hear a word against him. That was the trouble with Tremaron. They were so blindly loyal to each other, they couldn't see what was really going on – or more likely wouldn't admit it.

He remembered how no one had even questioned Pat Barley ferrying across all those enormous crates to Bloodhound Island a couple of months ago. To be fair, Alex had helped Ben and Kate solve that mystery, but it was at times like this that Alex's dogged belief in the innocence of all Tremarons could be irritating.

Mrs Cosham glanced at her watch impatiently. 'Nearly two and time for the arcade to open. Tracy-Anne'll have a fit. She's saving up for her wedding. Or so she says,' she added darkly.

'Here she comes,' said Alex. 'Watch out for trouble.'

Mrs Cosham's lips narrowed until they were simply a slit in her long, gloomy face.

Tracy-Anne was a tall girl with blonde hair piled up on the top of her head. She worked part-time on the cash desk in the arcade. Alex knew she had quarrelled with Mrs Cosham weeks ago and they no longer spoke. The argument had something to do with the tea rota between the magic shop and the arcade and had gathered pace, covering a wide range of grievances, past and present.

'Tell her Roy's gone,' Mrs Cosham said to Alex.

'Roy's gone,' said Alex to Tracy-Anne, who was already reading the notice in the window with rising indignation.

'Ask her where,' snapped Tracy-Anne.

'Where?' asked Alex automatically.

'Tell her I haven't the faintest and the family don't know either.'

'She hasn't the faintest and—' Alex began to repeat wearily.

'I *heard*.' Tracy-Anne was furious now. 'Holiday? He can't be on holiday. He makes his money out of holidays.'

'Ask her if she knows—' began Mrs Cosham.

'No I don't, you stupid old bat,' yelled Tracy-Anne. 'He owes me a week's wages and if I *did* know I'd tell you.'

'How dare you speak to me like that,' shouted Mrs Cosham. 'The trouble with you, young woman, is that you never had any manners. Roy Pearson is as honest a man as I've ever met.'

'Then you'd better meet a few more,' snapped Tracy-Anne. 'If you ask me, he's always been a bit of a crook.'

Alex, Ben and Kate began to edge cautiously away as the open warfare continued.

'Feel the heat,' said Alex.

'Can't someone negotiate a truce?' asked Ben.

'Not with those two. You'd need a UN peacekeeping force.'

Alex Banner was the youngest son of one of Tremaron's oldest fishing families and he was also Kate and Ben Lewis's best friend. They had arrived with their parents from London earlier in the year to take over Marlow House, a small hotel on the sea front, just behind the harbour.

At first they had been lonely, and if it hadn't

7

been for Alex's friendship they would have been lonelier still. Now after half a term at the local school, Ben and Kate knew a few more people, Marlow House had been completely redecorated and was doing good business, and the memories of London and their life in that distant city had begun to dim.

What was more, shortly after their arrival in Tremaron, Ben and Kate and Alex had solved the mystery of Bloodhound Island and this had given them some respect from the local community. Although they were still looked on as outsiders, the Lewises were slowly beginning to settle into the small Cornish seaside town.

As they walked through the narrow village streets that led up from the harbour, Kate and Ben were still curious about Roy Pearson and his abrupt disappearance.

'He never really wanted to be a fisherman,' said Alex sadly, for he loved the sea and was looking forward to the time when he could leave school and join his brothers on the family fishing boats. 'Roy always wanted to get out of Tremaron and make his fortune, but when he tried to leave he found he couldn't.'

'Was he arrested by the border guards?' asked Ben.

Alex took no notice of his teasing. 'Puts a spell

on you, this place. He went to London and came back in a couple of weeks because he was so homesick. So he decided to make his fortune here instead.'

'Here?' asked Kate, deliberately trying to wind Alex up. 'There's nothing here but fish.'

He carried on, ignoring her. 'One of his aunts had left him her boat and he sold it. Then the Roxy – the old cinema – closed down so he took on the lease and opened the magic shop on one side and the arcade in the rest of the place.'

'Who wants a magic shop in Tremaron?' asked Ben. 'I'd rather have a decent video store.'

'The magic shop may not get so many customers,' Alex admitted. 'But Tremaron's really gone for the arcade. Never had one of those in the town before. Lot of folks were against it but Roy got permission from the Council. Progress, they called it. Tourist amenities.' Alex paused reflectively. 'As for the magic – well, that was more of a hobby really. Roy always used to do tricks when he was a kid.'

'And now he's done another one,' said Ben. 'A vanishing trick.'

'Let's go and see Roy's brother,' said Kate. 'I'm sure we can find out where he is.' An inner voice told her that the fishing community would resent her interference, but she refused to listen to it. After all, people's jobs were at stake. Tracy-Anne and Mrs Cosham needed help – and she had also scented a new mystery.

'I don't think that would be a good idea,' began Alex unwillingly and Ben looked just as disapproving.

'Leave the relations out of it,' he said.

What was the matter with the boys, Kate wondered. Weren't they just being chicken? They had solved one mystery, hadn't they? So why couldn't they solve another?

'Does he live in the fishermen's cottages? What harm can it do?' Kate had a strong will and she soon managed to drag the information out of Alex who was looking increasingly uneasy.

'Their place is the last one down on the right, but they won't want us calling.' Alex sounded very uncomfortable. 'In fact, I think this is a really *bad* idea.'

'He's right,' agreed Ben. 'It's really none of our business—'

He never finished his sentence as Kate darted ahead, ringing the bell of a small white-washed cottage. After a short wait, the door was flung open by a giant of a man with long black hair and a deeply tanned and wrinkled face. He certainly didn't look at all pleased to see them. Even Alex.

'What do you lot want?'

'We just wondered if you knew where Roy was?' asked Kate, looking up at him hopefully. 'We went to the arcade and there's a notice on the door saying he's on holiday. Gone away for a while.'

'Ah.' There was an awkward silence during

which the frown on Mr Pearson's face deepened. 'Like the notice says – he's on his holidays,' he replied eventually. 'Now why don't you clear off?'

'We only want to help,' persisted Kate. 'His staff are worried and they don't know how to contact him.'

Mr Pearson stared at her angrily and she began to feel uncomfortable, wishing she hadn't ignored the boys and plunged in without thinking.

'Who do you think you are then?' said Mr Pearson sarcastically. 'The Flying Squad? Just because you got mixed up in that Bloodhound Island business doesn't give you the right to poke your nose into other folk's affairs. Now push off.' He slammed the door in their faces.

'He wasn't exactly friendly, was he?' said Ben. 'I didn't think he'd tell us anything. Why should he?'

'We *were* poking our noses in,' admitted Kate. 'It's my fault.' She wished she hadn't been so stupid.

'It's too late now,' snapped Alex, and they could see he was angry.

'Has he got a girl-friend?' asked Ben.

'He used to go out with Tracy-Anne, but they split up. Now she's got another bloke.'

'Do you think he's upset about that?'

13

'No,' said Alex with conviction. 'He's well rid of her. She's a right little stirrer.'

'Does he have any place he might go?' Kate was beginning to get back on the case again. 'Somewhere he might go to get away from pressure?'

Alex looked away. 'No,' he said. 'I haven't a clue.' It was as if he had suddenly decided to shut them out too.

What's he afraid of, wondered Ben. There's something he's not telling us. He and Kate had got to know Alex really well over the last few months and they could sense if he was holding out on them.

'Maybe there's some family trouble they're not letting on about—' suggested Kate quietly.

But Alex was not going to be drawn. 'We'd know if there was,' he said abruptly. 'Us fishermen stick together. I've got to get my tea now. See you.'

'Something makes me feel I've blown it,' said Kate as he hurried away.

'For once you're right,' Ben replied irritably.

Marlow House was only a small hotel, made up from four fishermen's cottages that had been knocked together. An extension round the back housed a kitchen and dining-room. The building

14

was white-washed and had big square windows that overlooked the harbour.

That night the dining-room was full and Ben and Kate were rushed off their feet. To make some pocket money they often worked in the hotel, and tonight they were helping to clear the tables.

'Couple of blokes asking about Roy Pearson out there,' said Bertha. She was a small, fiercely energetic woman who worked part-time in the village post office as well as coming in to 'give a hand' at Marlow House. 'Funny, isn't it?'

'Funny?' demanded Kate, helping to load the dishwasher. She had felt ashamed of herself earlier for upsetting the Pearsons and Alex, but now Bertha had suddenly brought the mystery alive again.

'I mean he takes a holiday for the first time in his life and then these two come nosing by.'

'Who are they?'

'Strangers,' Bertha said condemningly. 'At least one of them is. And Gerry Parks isn't much better. Hasn't been here since he was a kid.'

'We're strangers too, really.' Kate spoke her thoughts aloud, without really meaning to.

'You were.' Bertha was reassuring. 'But you're not now, you're Tremarons.'

'We won't be that for years,' she said

mournfully, and then smiled at Bertha, grateful for her kindness. 'Did you look in the visitors' book?'

'That's none of my business—' Bertha began.

'But *did* you look?' persisted Kate, knowing that she would have made it her business to check the two men out.

'I took a peek,' she admitted. 'I knew it was my duty – they come from Padstow. Business men of some kind.' She sniffed. 'Nabbed me in the hall. That Parks didn't even recognize me.'

'Really? What did they want?' asked Kate impatiently.

'They asked if I knew where Roy Pearson was. They'd been to the shop and the arcade and seen the notices, but they said they wanted to get hold of him urgently.'

'What for?'

'Don't know. I asked them – and they wouldn't say. So that's it then.' She looked at Kate curiously, hoping she knew something she didn't.

'I tell you what, I've got to go and clear their table. I'll see what I can find out.' She didn't mind offending strangers. It was just the local people Kate didn't like upsetting.

Before she went back to the dining-room, she

16

met Ben in the corridor, staggering back into the kitchen with yet another pile of dirty plates.

'You've got jam tart down your T-shirt,' she observed. 'And isn't there some more on your jeans?'

'I backed into the Littletons' table,' he replied. 'They weren't very pleased.'

'Bertha's been talking.'

'Does she ever stop? No wonder they call her Motor Mouth.'

'Actually she's just told me something rather interesting.'

When Kate had passed on what Bertha had found out, Ben said, 'Let's have a look at the visitors' book. Like now.'

'We'll have to move fast,' Kate warned him. 'Mum's in charge tonight. She won't want us slacking off.'

They slipped out furtively into reception and went through the book. Gerry Parks and Sam Tomson had checked in at Marlow House that afternoon, but they hadn't given the name of their company or even full addresses, except for the town of Padstow.

'Now you two,' said Mum, appearing noiselessly and making them jump. 'What are you doing?'

'Nothing,' they chorused guiltily.

'There's an awful lot of table clearing to be

done and I don't believe that's my job, is it?'

Ben and Kate hurried back to the dining-room as fast as they could. The last thing they wanted to do was put Mum in a bad mood and run the risk of being grounded. Not when there was mystery in the air.

'Shall I clear?' asked Kate. Parks and Tomson were middle-aged and wore expensive suits. Although they were overweight, they also looked tough. Maybe they're bailiffs, she thought. A couple had stayed at the hotel recently, men who were employed to take personal possessions from people who couldn't pay their bills. Could Roy Pearson have gone bankrupt? Was that why he had vanished and these men had arrived?

'OK,' said the slightly heavier-built of the two. 'You'll be the owners' daughter, will you?'

'Yes,' she replied evenly. 'I'm Kate.'

'And I'm Sam Tomson and this is my partner, Gerry Parks.' He gave her a friendly grin but his eyes were small and hard. 'We'll be staying for a few days.'

'Holiday?' she asked.

'Business. Do you know Roy Pearson at all?' He came straight to the point, catching Kate off guard.

'The man who runs the Roxy?'

'The very guy.'

'Hardly at all.'

'Does your brother?'

'He goes to the magic shop sometimes and we've both been to the arcade.'

'We're looking for Pearson,' said Parks. 'Be a help if you could give us a clue where he's gone.'

'Sorry. I've no idea,' replied Kate with deliberately irritating brightness. She didn't like either of them.

'Notice on the arcade door says he's on holiday.'

'Does it?'

'We saw his family. His mum and dad. Then we went to see his brother.'

'Yes?' Kate was determined to give nothing away.

'Seems to be a bit of a difference of opinion. His parents say he went to London. His brother's sure he's in Bristol. Strange, isn't it?'

Kate was clearing the plates now as fast as she could. 'Probably just a misunderstanding,' she said vaguely.

'Another odd thing though,' began Sam Tomson, watching her intently. 'Apparently you kids paid Mr Pearson a visit.'

'We were concerned about Roy—' Kate broke

off, realizing she had been led into a trap.

'I thought you didn't know him,' said Parks.

'We don't, but our friend does.'

'And who's your friend?'

Kate paused, feeling she was about to make a betrayal. But how could she refuse to give his name? 'Alex Banner,' she said reluctantly. 'He's known Roy all his life.'

Gerry smiled at her coldly. 'Doing a bit of snooping, were you?'

'We just went to see Roy's brother. In case we could help.'

'And he told you where he was,' suggested Sam Tomson threateningly.

'Of course not.' Kate was out of her depth, becoming increasingly uncomfortable.

Then Mum spotted what was happening and came hurrying over.

· 3 ·

'Is something wrong?' she asked anxiously.

'Not at all,' replied Gerry Parks smoothly. 'We were just congratulating your daughter on her local knowledge.'

'We've only been here a few months,' said Mum doubtfully.

'Long enough to make a hit,' said Sam Tomson. 'Lovely grub that was.'

'Well – thank you.' Slightly flustered and totally taken in, she stayed chatting to Parks and Tomson while Kate silently slipped away, managing to alert Ben who was in the kitchen.

'They're on to us,' she whispered.

While Bertha sang a selection of popular hymns, as she often did at this time of the evening, Kate took her brother into the corridor.

'I'm sure Alex's holding out on us. You know how close the fishing families are.'

'So close you can't prise them apart,' agreed Ben.

'And I don't like Parks and Tomson. They're heavies.'

'You can't tell by looks.' Ben was irritatingly superior now. 'They might be after him for some good reason,' he finished darkly.

'Roy comes from a fishing family,' began Kate feebly. She was still suffering from her encounter. The two men had been so purposeful, so frightening.

'You sound like Alex. Roy could still be a crook, whatever family he comes from. You just want him to be a hero. Those guys look like villains, so they have to *be* villains.'

'So you don't think anything's wrong,' Kate began sarcastically. 'Roy Pearson disappears. His staff don't know where he is. His family goes secretive and Alex backs off. Then a couple of thugs turn up as guests in our own hotel asking for him. That's just every-day life in Tremaron. According to you, anyway.'

'There's probably some perfectly ordinary explanation,' Ben said defensively.

'Like there was to Bloodhound Island?' she snapped.

'You'd make a mystery out of anything. You have to look at every angle.'

Kate answered her brother slowly, trying to keep calm and not lose her temper. 'By the time you've finished doing that, someone else will have solved it. Why don't you ring Alex? See if you can get any more out of him.'

'It'll be after nine when we're through here and Mum will expect—'

'She'll expect you to get stuck in like she did before.' Mrs Lewis was making another of her surprise appearances. 'What's got into you tonight?' she rapped out. 'Any more of this and you'll get the sack. Mr and Mrs Temple's table hasn't been cleared and they're both looking as if they'd like to find another hotel.'

Later, when the washing up was done, Ben went into the public call box in the corridor near reception, put some money in and dialled Alex's number. He knew that if he used the telephone in the family flat upstairs, Dad would be listening and getting curious.

Strictly speaking, they weren't allowed to make calls on this phone because it was for guests only, but Ben had waited until Mum was having a long gossip with Bertha and knew he was safe for a minute or two.

Mr Banner answered.

'It's Ben Lewis here. Could I speak to Alex?'

'That Sherlock Holmes on the job again?' he asked with heavy-handed humour. 'Or Hercule Poirot perhaps. OK, I'll get him providing you haven't got this phone bugged.' Mr Banner went away laughing.

'Listen,' said Ben when Alex eventually came on the line, 'there's two guys at the hotel, Parks and Tomson, and they've been asking Kate a load of questions about your mate Roy. They know we went round to his brother's and they think we know where he is. Do you?'

'No.' Alex sounded impatient.

'Do you think he's done a runner?' Ben was determined to press on.

'Who from? The Mafia?'

'From bailiffs or – or someone.' He knew he sounded lame.

'He's as honest as the day,' said Alex indignantly.

Well – you would say that, wouldn't you,

24

thought Ben. 'Tracy-Anne didn't think so.'

'I told you – she's a right little stirrer.'

'They're really heavy, these guys,' persisted Ben. 'They could do Roy some harm.'

'He can look after himself.' Alex sounded defensive now, as if he could tell Ben more if he wanted to. He obviously didn't.

'Are you sure you don't know where he is?' he asked bluntly.

'No.'

'OK. If you say so.' Ben sighed.

'You can't make a mystery out of everything,' said Alex. 'Just because we solved one doesn't mean you can set up a detective agency.'

'Oh I wasn't thinking of doing that,' replied Ben quickly. 'Not while I'm working for Scotland Yard.' He rang off, remembering guiltily how superior he had been to his sister on exactly the same subject. Ben stood staring down at the phone, realizing he and Kate were soon going to earn the reputation of being Tremaron's busiest busybodies.

As he left the phone box, with a nasty start Ben caught sight of Sam Tomson's bulky and menacing figure in the semi-darkness of the hallway. What had he heard?

'Had a chat with your sister earlier,' Tomson said in a confiding tone. 'About Roy Pearson.'

'Yes?'

'Thought I heard his name just then.'

'Where?' asked Ben, looking around him, deliberately puzzled.

'When you were talking to your mate on the phone.'

'You were listening to my call—'

'Couldn't help it. Not with you bellowing your head off.'

'I wasn't talking about Roy Pearson. Why should I?'

'That's for you to tell me.' Tomson was smiling in the dark, a cat-like grin that was particularly unpleasant. 'What are you kids up to, eh?'

'Nothing.'

'Just listen to me. This Roy Pearson – he's no good. A right villain and now he's done a runner.'

'Who are you? The police?' demanded Ben.

'No.' Tomson drew back a little, aware that he had overstepped the mark. 'We've got business interests in his affairs and that's all I'm prepared to say. But I give you fair warning that you're dealing with a nasty bit of work and he could come after you.'

'Why?' asked Ben fearfully.

'Because you know where he is, don't you? And he won't like that. Why don't you tell us and we can take care of him. See you and your sister come to no harm.' There was an edge to Tomson's voice now and the heavy, cat-like grin had disappeared.

'Of course I don't know where he is.'

'Does your mate?'

Ben decided the time had come to be assertive. 'If you don't leave me and my sister alone,' he said rather shakily, 'I'll speak to my parents.'

'Don't take that tone with me, young man,' said Tomson softly. 'I'm only trying to warn you.'

Ben hurried up the stairs to the family flat, but paused, crouching down on the landing as he heard Gerry Parks's voice below. He had just come out of the restaurant and obviously hadn't heard their conversation.

'We'll be late for Tracy-Anne,' he babbled before Sam Tomson could stop him. 'She's sure Pearson's in those caves and maybe she knows—'

'Shut up,' whispered Sam Tomson. 'Just shut up.'

Kate was waiting for Ben in the spare room with her case book. Their parents had agreed they could use the space to do their homework.

Little did they realize the room had become a headquarters.

Sitting on the edge of the bed, Ben told Kate about his phone call to Alex, what had happened between him and Tomson and, more importantly, what he had just overheard.

'The caves,' she muttered and went to the bookcase. 'Dad gave me this local guide ages ago.' She thumbed over the pages and then said, 'Caves. The caves in Tremaron are called the Shadow Caves.' She briefly scanned the page while Ben watched her impatiently.

'What does it mean – Shadow Caves?' he asked eventually. Was she going on reading for ever?

'It's part of a Tremaron legend. Apparently the smugglers used the caves to hide contraband from the Excisemen, setting up a trap for them if they made a raid. This book doesn't say what the trap was but apparently the Excisemen drowned in the caves. The legend has it that you can still see their shadows on the walls of the caves, day or night, trying to escape the tide.'

'Isn't there an explanation for the shadows as well?' asked Ben hopefully.

'Something about light flooding down narrow chimneys inside the cliff and flickering on water that reflects on the rock. There's always an explanation, isn't there? To spoil things.' Kate paused. 'So what are we going to do then?'

'Persuade Alex to talk to us. I'm sure he knows more than he's letting on.' Ben sounded much more positive now and she was immediately relieved. At least he didn't still think she was making it all up.

Ben was more cautious than she was, but once he had made up his mind he would always follow through to the end. Although they often rubbed each other up the wrong way, Kate knew they made a good team.

'What if Alex won't talk?' she asked.

'Then we'll ask around Tremaron. We'll have to be careful though. Parks and Tomson are going to be watching every move we make.'

Kate sighed. 'If only Alex was here sharing it all with us. I miss him. As for asking around Tremaron, you might as well try getting into Fort Knox.'

'It'll take a lot to win Alex round now,' said Ben despondently. 'We might have to solve this mystery on our own.'

Later, acting on impulse, Ben slipped out of Marlow House to see if Parks and Tomson were still around. He had a hunch they might have gone down to The Ship's Wheel, a small pub further down the street.

Ben sauntered along, trying to appear casual. When he arrived outside the pub he checked carefully that no one was looking before gazing in at the window. Sure enough, he was right; through the smoke he could just make out Parks and Tomson. But they had a companion.

Sitting at a table in an alcove, Tracy-Anne was holding a drink, talking fast, a malicious grin on her doll-like face.

Did Tracy-Anne really know that Roy Pearson was hiding out in the Shadow Caves? What *was* she telling Parks and Tomson?

Sadly, Ben knew he had no way of finding out and soon he crept cautiously away, returning to Marlow House and reporting back to Kate.

'Alex said she was a stirrer,' she said when he had finished. 'I bet you that's exactly what she's doing now.'

Ben found sleep difficult that night, tossing and turning, his mind full of the Shadow Caves and the ghosts of the Excisemen trying to escape from the tide.

Kate, too, was finding it hard to sleep, but for a different reason. Did Alex really know something they didn't? Who *were* Gerry Parks and Sam Tomson and why were they so threatening? And what exactly was Tracy-Anne telling them?

The questions hammered on, but eventually Kate drifted off into a light and restless sleep.

· 4 ·

The day was blustery and overcast as Kate and Ben slouched through the narrow winding streets, out of sorts with themselves and dreading meeting Alex in case he was unfriendly. They felt isolated, newcomers once more, and were beginning to wonder if they were not in the same league as Parks and Tomson: interfering strangers who were trying to force their way into a closed community.

They had also begun to bicker, not knowing

how to cope with the situation.

'You're always too impulsive,' Ben was saying. 'You never think ahead.'

'You don't get off your backside fast enough,' she told him frankly. 'If a couple of masked men were standing outside the post office on a dark night you'd want to check if anyone was giving a fancy dress party before calling the police.'

'Excuse me.' The voice was brisk and full of authority.

They turned round to see a young girl staring at them. She was about Ben's age and had a tanned face, green eyes and a crop of mousy hair. Ben thought she was vaguely familiar and then realized he must have seen her at school, although she wasn't in any of his classes.

'Aren't you Ben and Kate Lewis? I'm Emily Pearson. Roy's niece. I just wondered if I could have a word with you.'

'Sure,' said Ben. He didn't know how to react and this girl seemed incredibly forceful.

'A private word,' Emily said meaningfully, looking around the busy street uneasily.

'Where can we go?' Kate was hostile, not wanting to be ordered about, but her curiosity was getting the better of her as usual.

'Follow me, but keep your distance. Don't look as if you know me. We'll talk in the old fish store up on the hill,' she added.

Kate and Ben dutifully followed Emily Pearson
for some way. She was short and strongly built
and looked casually confident as she swung her
shopping bag. Ben felt much less at ease and
kept glancing around nervously.

'Stop looking back,' hissed Kate. 'You'll make
us seem suspicious.'

'We *are* suspicious,' he muttered. 'Following
that girl as if we're special agents. It's
ridiculous.'

'Try and look as if you're out for a stroll.'

'We *never* go out for a stroll,' Ben reminded her.
'Like Roy Pearson never goes on holiday.'

Eventually they reached the old tumbledown
fish store which stood in an overgrown
wilderness of spiky undergrowth. The door hung
slightly ajar and Emily walked straight in.

Inside the fishy smell still predominated and it
was so dark that Kate and Ben could hardly see.
Then her disembodied voice said, 'Now we can
talk. I know you came to see my dad with Alex.'

'It was a stupid thing to have done,' said Ben.
'We shouldn't have interfered.'

'How come?' Emily asked in surprise, and then
added, 'Who says?'

'Alex,' said Kate.

'Oh him,' she replied dismissively. 'A lot of people round here want to cover up for Roy. I'm not sure why.' She paused. 'I don't think he should be left to run off like that. He could be in real danger, and what's more, that Tracy-Anne's been spreading rumours, saying he's taken all the cash from the arcade, including her and Mrs Cosham's wages.'

'She didn't say that when we saw her yesterday,' said Ben.

'Well, she is now.'

'What about Mrs Cosham?' asked Kate. 'What does she reckon?'

'She's bound to say the opposite to Tracy-Anne. Anyway, she's blind loyal to Roy.'

'Why do *you* reckon Roy took off?' asked Ben.

'I don't rightly know, but he's been pretty upset for a few days now. Then he suddenly said he was going for a holiday, but of course he wasn't because he never does. Mum and Dad know something but they're not telling me, and I reckon young Alex's parents have told him a tale or two that he's not passing on. But the main problem is Tracy-Anne. The whole town's beginning to believe her.'

'That Roy did a runner with the cash?' Ben looked surprised. 'I thought the fishing families always stuck together.'

'They do,' said Emily fiercely, 'but what about the others? Tracy-Anne's telling everyone she thinks he's hiding out in the Shadow Caves.'

'How does she know?' demanded Kate.

'She doesn't,' replied Emily. 'She's just putting the boot in. The caves used to be his favourite haunt.'

Kate looked doubtful. 'If he *had* done a runner, he wouldn't be hanging about in there, would he?' Then she paused. 'Do *you* think he took the cash?'

'Of course not.' Emily looked horrified at the idea, but Kate wondered if she was like Mrs Cosham, blind loyal to Roy. 'What's more,' Emily continued, 'those men are here, asking for him. I've seen them and I'm really scared for him.'

'*They* wouldn't go after him in the caves, would they?' asked Kate.

'I wouldn't like to bet on that.' Emily was anxious. 'Gerry Parks used to live here years ago, when he was a boy, so he might know the layout. He could drown Roy in the tide like the Excisemen. Someone ought to warn him.' She was close to tears now; all her former confidence seemed to have disappeared.

'Why don't you tell your parents then?' asked Ben.

'They wouldn't listen to me. I think they reckon Roy should hide out for a while, but I don't know why.' She sounded genuinely mystified. 'Look – you've *got* to help me.' Emily was obviously desperate to convince them.

'What do you want us to do?' Kate asked quietly.

She began to speak fast. Too fast. 'We can get down on the beach this afternoon. It's low tide and at least we could check the caves out,' she pleaded. 'I know the layout. I won't get you into any danger, I promise.'

'Suppose we're seen by Parks and Tomson?' said Ben. 'They're already suspicious.'

'That's OK. They've just driven off somewhere.' Emily paused. 'Anyway, we can reach the caves without going near a road. My mum'll kill me if I go alone. *Please* come with me,' she pleaded. But they both noticed that underneath the pleading was a powerful driving force.

'All right,' said Kate, exchanging a glance with Ben. 'We'll meet you here about two.'

'We've got to be careful we're not seen.' Again her brother was more cautious. 'And we're not going far into those caves.'

He knew deep down they were making a big mistake, but because he had been made to feel an outsider Ben wanted to get his own back on Alex and try to crack the mystery. He knew Kate felt the same.

'You won't let me down?' Emily was looking unsure of them now.

'No,' said Ben. 'We won't let you down.'

They walked slowly back to Marlow House in silence, preoccupied with their own thoughts. Was Roy Pearson hiding in the Shadow Caves, or had he done a runner with the money and was now hundreds of miles away, never to be seen again?

Of course, there was always the other option – that Roy was a completely innocent man, taking an unexpected break.

'Wait a minute.' Kate grabbed her brother's arm, dragging him into a passage that ran down the side of Marlow House.

As she did so, a large Volvo glided round the corner and pulled up in front of the hotel. Sam Tomson was at the wheel with Tracy-Anne beside him; Gerry Parks was in the back.

As she clambered out, Tracy-Anne said pertly, 'Thanks for the ride. I enjoyed that.'

'I hope you haven't been taking *us* for a ride, Tracy-Anne,' Parks warned.

'Now why should I do a thing like that?' she

simpered. 'That wouldn't be in my best interests, would it? Just think over what I've said. Those caves are definitely worth checking. It would be just like Roy not to go too far away from Tremaron.'

'How well do you *really* know the layout, Gerry?' asked Tomson and Parks looked doubtful.

'Not that well and *I* don't want to go in there. Are you sure that's where he is?' He began to back off, clearly afraid.

'You won't get a word out of those fishermen, so it's no good asking them. And you're right – those interfering kids know something.' Tracy-Anne began to flounce off down the high street.

'We're very grateful.' Sam Tomson was giving her an admiring look. 'We'll be in touch.'

As the two men went back into Marlow House, Kate turned to Ben. 'Let's follow her,' she said with her usual impulsiveness. This time, however, Ben was quick to agree.

Making sure they were unobserved, they kept her at a distance. Fortunately Tracy-Anne didn't look back. She was a distinctive figure in her blue miniskirt, her high heels clacking over the cracked pavements.

Tracy-Anne struggled on round the harbour wall and along the coast road that gradually wound its way up the cliff. Then she turned down a small and rutted lane.

Kate and Ben hung back until she was well out of sight.

Happy View Caravan Park overlooked the sea and contained a motley collection of mobile homes with names like Dunroamin, The Nook and Seaspray.

Keeping their backs to a brick wall that enclosed the headland, Ben and Kate saw Tracy-Anne climbing up the steps of a small, battered caravan. As she did so, a man opened the door and she hurried inside.

'Could you make out who that was?' asked Kate.

'Just some bloke.'

'That all? You don't – you don't think he could be Roy?'

'After all she said about him?' Ben looked doubtful.

'She could have been bluffing.'

'Why?'

Kate shrugged. 'I don't know. Let's try and take a closer look,' she suggested.

Just as they were about to move cautiously around the edge of the site, a woman appeared from a small office, wearing overalls.

'What do you two want?' she demanded.

'We – er – we wondered – our parents wanted to know if there were any caravans to let.'

She looked at them as if they were potential vandals. 'This is an owners' site only. There's no lets, summer or winter. Now why don't you clear off?'

'What are we going to do?' asked Ben as they sat in the spare room after lunch to talk the mystery over.

Kate had written up the clues they had so far in her case book, but even she had to admit they didn't amount to much yet.

'Go along with Emily?' she suggested.

'We'd be crazy to explore those caves.' Ben seemed to have taken against the whole idea now.

'We can't let her down.' Kate was anxious to hang on to Emily's proposal. It seemed their only way forward and surely she wasn't going to be stupid enough to run them all into danger.

'We can meet her and explain.'

'That we're too chicken to go with her?'

'If necessary,' said Ben resolutely. 'But it's not really a question of being chicken. Just being sensible.'

Kate's curiosity, however, was running out of

control and she had never liked the word 'sensible'. 'We won't go in far. Do you want to solve this mystery or not?'

'You know I do.' He paused. 'But how do we *know* Roy Pearson's in the Shadow Caves?'

'We don't,' said Kate. 'That's the point. But Emily's a local so she could be right. Besides – she's so insistent. I get the feeling she's desperate for us to go with her, that she's got a pretty good idea he's in there.'

'I wouldn't take a bet on that,' Ben said cautiously.

'I would,' said Kate. 'It's our only chance. So what are you going to do? Leave it to me and Emily?'

'No,' he replied huffily. 'I wouldn't do that.'

Kate knew she had won.

· 5 ·

Emily led them over the headland and down a
narrow track that became so steep they could
only make slow progress. The clay had been
turned into muddy rivulets by recent rain, and
below them the sea churned, a cold grey-green,
heaving at the shore, the tide reluctantly edging
back to leave a widening strip of smooth sand.

The cliffs were high, enclosing the cove, and
they could already see the mouths of the caves
on the far side, dark gashes in the rock face.

'Watch your step,' said Emily as Ben slipped past her, grabbing at a tree root and steadying himself. 'It can be treacherous after the rain.'

He nodded. 'I'd noticed,' he said, wiping the mud off his hands.

Kate was aware that Emily's confidence had returned. Could Emily be playing some kind of game with them? Why did she really need them to go to the Shadow Caves with her? Why was she still clutching her shopping bag? Above all, shouldn't they confide in her completely, share everything they had discovered so far? Yet some instinct held Kate back and she was sure Ben felt the same.

The path became steeper and soon they were all clinging to trees and bushes as they inched their way down to the beach over the slippery surface.

The wind was getting up now, howling eerily, and out at sea Kate could see white horses.

'What's that?' gasped Ben.

'It's like someone singing.' Kate was terrified, the little hairs standing up on the back of her neck.

'That's the sea song,' said Emily. 'It just means the tide's going out in the caves.'

The sound was weird. A kind of tinkling sighing that constantly changed note and pace, rather like a waterfall with giant ice cubes.

'I don't really know why it makes that noise,' said Emily. 'Maybe it's to do with the rock formation. But it's strange, isn't it?'

Ben shivered. 'It's really eerie.'

They waited a little longer, listening to the haunting sound until, with one last tinkling rush, it disappeared.

'We're going to have to jump this last bit. The path's been worn away,' said Emily.

She landed neatly and athletically in the sand. Ben was close behind her, but Kate misjudged the distance and fell headlong. As she picked herself up she gazed round the steep-sided cove and felt much more apprehensive.

The rocks seemed dark and menacing, and the waves were licking malevolently at the beach, as if they were waiting to surge up and drown them all.

'This cove gives me the creeps,' said Ben. 'What's it called?'

'All Souls,' said Emily.

'Drowned souls more likely,' he muttered. 'How long have we got?' he asked anxiously.

'To live?' said Kate.

'Before the tide comes in, idiot,' Ben snapped.

'A couple of hours,' Emily replied. 'It should be

more than enough.'

She didn't sound reassuring.

As they walked across the flat wet sand to the caves, Kate had a dreadful premonition that Emily was deliberately leading them into a trap. She tried to throw it off, telling herself there was no reason for Emily to do such a thing, but the feeling persisted as they began to clamber over some ridges of rock that were hard up against the cliff. They made a natural bridge over a lower series of dark cave mouths that smelt of seaweed and something pungent they couldn't identify. Then, suddenly, a gull flew out of a crevice in the rock, screaming raucously, its eyes venomous, furious at being disturbed.

'No one comes here for months at a time,' said Emily. 'The gulls aren't used to people.'

Kate gave a little cry of fear as she almost stepped on the moving shell of a giant spider crab that was scuttling sideways across the ledge.

'Got left by the tide,' said Emily. 'Like a lot of other creatures round here.'

Ben was getting tired of her throw-away comments. Was she deliberately trying to wind them up?

The cave mouth Emily chose seemed incredibly small, and the idea of entering the foul-smelling place was repellent.

'We can't go in there,' Ben sounded adamant.

'No chance,' added Kate.

Emily however was already squeezing inside. 'Don't worry,' she called back to them. 'You can stand up after a couple of metres and I've got a torch.' Rummaging in her bag she pulled it out and switched on the powerful beam.

'There's no guarantee Roy's even going to be here,' muttered Kate as she ducked down into the rocky cavity, following the torch beam but soon banging her head.

'Watch it,' called Emily.

Now she tells me, thought Kate. 'You OK?' she shouted back to Ben.

'I wouldn't yell like that,' he replied acidly. 'You might bring the roof down.' Now he was even more certain they had been incredibly foolish to offer to help Emily.

Slowly, the cave got broader and higher until they arrived in a huge cavern, dimly lit from above. Water dripped down one of the walls, there were great smudges of damp clay on the others but the place had an incredible beauty, still and silent as a cathedral.

'It's amazing,' said Ben, forgetting his fears for a moment, overwhelmed by the majesty of it all.

'Now you can see why Roy loves the Shadow

Caves,' said Emily, her voice trembling slightly. 'I *know* he's in the network somewhere.'

'Network?' asked Kate. The word sounded ominous.

'The tunnels lead right back into the cliffs – a couple of miles or more.'

'Are we above the tide-line here?' asked Ben.

'Not yet.'

'Where are we going then?' snapped Kate. 'I mean – we could get lost and you don't know the way—'

'But I do,' she said confidently. 'I've been right up to the top galleries with Roy. It won't take us long, I promise.'

'*How* long?' demanded Ben.

'Half an hour at the outside. We'll easily beat the tide.'

'You sure?' asked Kate nervously, but Emily was already darting ahead.

· 6 ·

'We'll have to go up a chimney,' Emily casually informed them when they caught up with her. 'I'll go first. It's quite easy,' she added, annoying them with her superior attitude.

She had led them to the back of the cavern where the roof was much lower. Gazing up, Ben could only see a narrow shaft snaking into the rock.

'We should come out in the third layer of galleries,' Emily was saying. 'All you do is just brace your body against the sides and climb.'

'Any light up there?' asked Kate grimly.

'Not much – but we've got the torch.' Emily began to pull at a mound of debris, and shale cascaded to the floor in a miniature landslide.

Emily was right. It was really quite easy to climb the chimney. Kate and Ben did as they had been told, bracing themselves against the rock, finding plenty of footholds and handholds, the torch a bright glimmer above them.

Eventually, they emerged breathless at the top, and when Emily flashed her torch around Ben and Kate could see that they were standing in a narrow tunnel, the roof almost touching their heads.

'I thought you said we'd come out into caves, not a tunnel,' said Kate.

'It's so low here we can hardly stand up,' complained Ben. 'And apart from the torch there's no light at all. Hadn't we better go back? We must have come up the wrong chimney.' Any trust Emily had inspired in him on the climb up suddenly plummeted.

'We're *fine*,' she said rather vaguely. 'I know where we are.'

As Emily spoke they heard a fluttering sound and something soared over Kate's shoulder with an echoing squeak. A restless dry rustling followed which was particularly unpleasant.

Trying to steady herself, Kate reached up, plunging her hand into soft fur.

'The roof's moving,' she yelped, staggering back.

Emily's torch swept upwards. 'They're only bats,' she said scornfully. 'You mustn't upset them.'

Ben thought he was going to be sick as he gazed up at the soft ceiling of furry mouse-like bats hanging upside down.

'I can't go on,' said Kate, shaking all over, but Emily didn't seem the least bit worried.

'It's incredible,' she said. 'I've never seen so many roosting together. I wonder if Roy knows about this.'

'So you haven't been here before. We *did* come up the wrong chimney,' said Kate accusingly, trying to recover from her fright.

'So what if we did? I know what I'm doing.' But Emily's voice rang with a false confidence now.

'Bet you don't.' Kate glared at her in the semi-darkness, furious with herself for not listening to Ben and landing them in such danger.

Then Ben stumbled on the uneven floor of the tunnel. 'Shine that torch down here,' he said

53

urgently. In the strong beam, the grease-proof packet appeared pallid, like some kind of fungoid growth. When Ben picked it up he discovered inside half a ham sandwich with a large bite taken out of the middle.

'It's only slightly stale,' he said, fingering the bread.

Emily hugged her shopping bag joyfully. 'What did I tell you? He *is* here after all.'

'Well someone's been around. Not necessarily Roy,' said Ben.

'What's in that bag of yours, Emily?' asked Kate with sudden suspicion.

'None of your business.'

'It *is* our business. You practically forced us here in the first place. I want to know what you're *really* up to.' She grabbed Emily's bag and wrenched it open. 'Come on, then,' she yelled. 'Shine your torch in here.'

As she reluctantly co-operated, Kate dragged out a large packet of sandwiches and a thermos.

'That's thoughtful of you,' she said. 'A picnic. We've had lunch but tea would be nice.'

'It's food for Roy,' Emily replied stubbornly. 'I *know* he's here. I was just too scared to come on my own.'

'What about Alex?' asked Kate. 'Why didn't you get *him* to go with you? He must know the layout better than you. Why are we the mugs?'

'I wouldn't come up here with Alex. He believes in the shadow ghosts.'

'And we don't?' asked Ben.

'You aren't locals,' persisted Emily. 'Don't you see? They're *all* superstitious.'

'Why don't you come clean with us?' said Ben, slightly mollified. 'Was this all pre-arranged? Are you going to meet Roy?'

'No.' Emily shook her head. 'It's just a hunch and—'

Kate grabbed Ben's arm. 'Someone's coming up the chimney,' she whispered.

As the bats began to flutter, they heard a gasping sound in the narrow shaft.

'It can't be Roy,' whispered Emily. 'He'd never be puffing and blowing like that.'

'Let's move.' Kate was making the decisions now and they stumbled on down the tunnel, the torch muffled in Emily's bag. Meanwhile, the grunting and groaning became louder.

Eventually they came to a divide and the tunnel split into two.

'Which way?' whispered Kate.

Suddenly all Emily's sense of direction disappeared. 'I'm not sure if I *have* been in this network before,' she admitted.

'Now you tell us.' Ben was furious.

'This isn't the moment for arguing.' Kate was longing to creep back and try and see round the corner but knew she couldn't take the risk. 'Whoever it was must be out of the tunnel by now and coming towards us,' she hissed urgently.

Grabbing the torch from Emily, Ben focused the beam on the roof for what seemed the most unbearable length of time.

'There's a ledge up there,' he said at last. 'We might just get on it.'

'What about the bats?' asked Emily. 'There might be a lot of them up there.'

'Too bad. They'll have to move over. Take the torch, I'm going for it.'

Ben reached up, hauling himself on to the ledge, and beckoned the others to follow.

To his and Kate's great relief there weren't any furry bodies to cuddle up to and there was just room for them all to squeeze together.

A powerful torch beam swept the tunnel as a figure stumbled past, hunched and squat, creepily reminding them of the ghostly Excisemen. They heard a grunt, a muffled curse and then the bulky shadow took the left-hand turn.

'We've got to go back the way we came,' Kate whispered after a few seconds.

'What about Roy?' Emily was stubborn. 'I'm sure that was Gerry Parks. He might really hurt him.'

'Parks could really hurt us,' muttered Kate.

'I'm not going back. Not till I find him. You two can go if you want,' said Emily.

'We can't leave you here alone.'

'We'll take the right-hand passage and see where it goes. At least we've got a fifty per cent chance of success.' Then Ben suddenly had an unpleasant thought. 'If the passage is circular we could run straight into Gerry Parks. What would we say to him?'

'Ask him if he's found Roy Pearson,' Kate suggested.

· 7 ·

A sudden bellowing cry broke the deep velvet silence, followed by stumbling footsteps. Fortunately they had not yet climbed down from the ledge.

No one moved a muscle as Gerry Parks ran back below them, whimpering with fear. He tripped, dropped his torch, picked it up again and sped on.

'What was that all about?' whispered Ben.

'Parks must have seen something – someone –

down that passage,' said Kate slowly and fearfully.

They gazed at each other in dismay, listening to Gerry Parks's wheezing gasps as he bumped painfully down the chimney.

'Shadows, maybe. Ghosts, no,' said Ben firmly, inching himself off the ledge and jumping down.

'Where are we going?' asked Kate.

'We've got to check out what Parks saw.'

'Do we have to?' asked Emily unwillingly.

'Of course we do.' Ben was determined. 'If you want to find Roy, that is.'

They hurried cautiously down the tunnel which, to their horror, soon became so narrow that they were barely able to scrape through. Parks must have had a difficult job, thought Kate.

Gradually they became aware of a dim glow as the passage broadened out into a small cave. They came to an abrupt halt, seeing shadows that looked horribly human moving across the wall, deadly purposeful in the fitful glimmer.

'The Excisemen,' Ben gulped. 'The shadow ghosts.'

'It's just light,' said Kate, trying to pull herself together. 'Light reflecting on water,' she added.

'The tide?' He still wasn't thinking straight

and Emily was shaking so hard it was as if she had suddenly contracted a fever.

'How could it be the tide up here? It's some kind of natural water course through the rock, and the light on it's making the shadows move.'

'They *look* like ghosts,' gulped Emily.

'They look like anything you want them to look like,' explained Kate impatiently.

Ben was staring ahead unbelievingly. 'What's that lying on the ground by the stream?'

'It's a skeleton,' shrieked Emily, standing stock still.

Ben forced himself to walk hesitantly towards what appeared to be a pile of bleached bones. He stood for a long while staring down at them.

'What are you doing?' To her annoyance, Kate's voice was shrill.

Then Ben began to laugh.

'What's so funny?' asked Kate, the shock waves beginning to subside.

'This skeleton's made of plastic,' he said, 'and there's a label on it which says: *With the Compliments of Roy Pearson's Magic Shop*.'

'Is that meant to be a *joke*?' Kate felt a surge of real anger for the absent Roy.

'Or a warning—'

'Parks was fooled all right,' said Emily with satisfaction, her confidence returning. 'Are you there, Roy?' she called, and her voice echoed round the cavern mockingly.

When it faded there was a deepening hush in which they could only hear the faint gurgle of water surging through the narrow channel to the sea.

Ben glanced at his watch. 'If you're right about the tide, Emily, then we've got about forty-five minutes left before it turns.'

'Let's take a last look,' she said, grabbing back the torch and flashing it around the interior of the cavern.

The beam only lit black rock on which water glistened.

Surely we can go back down the chimney now, hoped Kate, suddenly desperate for safety and glorious fresh air, but to her dismay she sensed that the others had got a second wind.

'Wait a minute. What's that up there?' Ben was gazing up at the wall.

'It's an arrow carved in the rock,' said Kate sharply. 'Probably another of Roy's tricks.'

'I don't think so. It's filled with moss which means the arrow's been around a long time. Look – there's another one over there.'

Emily flashed her torch around again, lighting more arrows in the rock, fainter but still possible to make out. Above them was the carved inscription: TEMPUS FUGIT.

'I think it means time flies,' explained Ben.

'It certainly ran out for the Excisemen, but we've still got some left.' Emily swept her torch along the cave wall. Sure enough, there were more arrows which led to some crudely carved lettering that didn't make any sense at all. The three of them read it again and again. WALLIS ANDREW LOVES LOUISE STAFFORD. WESLEY INSTEP LOVES LUCY. MURRAY OFTEN VOTES EARLY.

'It's nonsense,' said Kate dismissively. 'Let's be getting back.'

'Wait a minute,' said Emily. 'Suppose it's some kind of code?'

Kate tried hard to concentrate but failed, all the time wondering if she could hear the sound of Gerry Parks's returning footsteps. Gradually, however, her reasoning powers returned. 'What about the last letter of each word?' she suggested.

'SWSED YPSY YNSY,' said Ben eventually. 'Makes a lot of sense.'

'Try the first then.'

'WALLS WILL MOVE. That doesn't make so much sense either. They look pretty solid round here.'

They all stared blankly round the cave,

wondering what to do next.

'Let's try over there. By the last letter of the final word,' suggested Emily, reaching up and pushing at the damp rock, but nothing happened.

'What about the very first letter?' Ben pushed and pulled. Still nothing happened.

'It's just some kind of joke,' said Kate and Emily frowned.

'The arrow stops just here,' said Ben and pushed hard.

'We're wasting time,' Kate began, desperate to go now.

As she spoke, a small section of rock slowly opened outwards with a slight grinding sound.

'Walls will move,' muttered Ben. 'I wonder why.'

A flight of stone steps descended into darkness and they stared down fearfully, the damp, shut-in smell almost choking them, their ears filled with the ominous lapping of water.

'I've got to go down.' Emily's voice trembled. 'Don't leave me. I can't face it on my own.' She looked up at Ben pleadingly.

'Did you know about this?' demanded Kate. 'It wasn't the wrong chimney, was it? You were looking for this all the time.'

There was a long silence while they stared at each other in the semi-darkness. Emily was the first to look away.

'I wasn't sure,' she began. 'Roy told me this place existed but nothing else.'

'Why *are* you so desperate to find him?' demanded Kate, knowing that if they cross-examined her much more she would probably break down. But Kate couldn't stop herself; she had to discover what Emily knew. 'The more I think about it the more I realize how dangerous all this is,' she said accusingly. 'You've just dropped us in it.'

'We want to be your friends,' said Ben quietly. 'If we're going to help you, you must try and trust us.'

'I've *got* to find him.' Emily's green eyes were full of tears. 'Most of Tremaron see Roy as a failure. He's never made any money, the business has always been just about to collapse and now he's done a runner. That Tracy-Anne – she's hated Roy ever since he dumped her. Now she's spreading these rumours about him taking the money.'

'But what can you achieve by tracking him down here?' asked Ben.

'I want him to come back and face them all. Prove he didn't take the money. Stand up to his debtors and try and sort it all out.'

'And you reckon you can convince him?'

'We've always been close. Do you believe me?' She turned to face them in the murky light and both Kate and Ben felt relieved. They were convinced she was telling the truth now.

'Yes,' said Ben. 'But we know something *you* should know.'

'What is it?' Emily immediately looked alarmed.

He went on to describe how he had seen Tracy-Anne with Parks and Tomson in the pub and then getting out of their car the following day.

'Then we tailed her to the caravan site,' Kate continued. 'There was a man there.' She hesitated. 'We wondered if it was Roy.'

'No way,' said Emily contemptuously. 'He'd never go and stay with *her*.'

'How much money do you think there was at the arcade?' asked Kate. 'You say the business was doing badly. Would there have been much cash there?'

'There might have been,' Emily replied and paused. 'Roy's no crook but he's not much of a business man either. He used to keep money in the arcade for a long time. He kept forgetting to go to the bank.'

'Convenient,' muttered Kate.

'I tell you – he's not a crook,' yelled Emily.

'Keep your voice down,' Ben advised her. 'Gerry Parks might bring back Sam Tomson to hold his hand. What about Parks and Tomson? Do you reckon they know about the sliding rock?'

'Parks never even got past Roy's plastic skeleton,' Emily replied. 'They don't have a clue.' She stared down the roughly-hewn steps again. 'Do you reckon Roy could be hiding down there somewhere?'

Ben knew the risk they would have to take, but they had come so far they couldn't back out now. 'We'll take a look,' he said.

'Don't be so crazy. This must be the smugglers' trap,' whispered Kate. 'And we're walking straight into it.'

'We've *got* to find Roy,' insisted Emily. 'Please don't leave me. I don't want to go down there either, but I've got to check it out.'

'We'll go down,' said Ben. 'Just a short way.'

'All right,' agreed Kate reluctantly, knowing they were taking the biggest risk of their lives.

Slowly Emily began to climb down, her torch sweeping each step, the sound of the lapping water below much louder and more menacing.

Cautiously, Kate and Ben followed.

The beam lit more faintly carved arrows on the walls.

Kate glanced at her watch. 'The tide should be on the turn now. We'll just carry on for another thirty steps, then we'll turn round. OK, Emily?'

But she didn't reply.

This is like entering a tomb, thought Ben as they climbed on down. He tried hard to banish the idea, but it wouldn't go away.

Kate was counting. 'Fourteen, fifteen, sixteen, seventeen—'

'These steps are damp,' said Emily suddenly, her voice flat and miserable, realizing that, after all this, they must be on a false trail.

'They're getting damper,' Kate pointed out. 'Twenty-five, twenty-six, twenty—'

The torch picked out the sheet of black rippling water barring their way, lazily lapping the steps.

'OK,' said Ben. 'That's it.' This was definitely the trap the smugglers had prepared for the Excisemen and he didn't want to hang around any longer. Even Emily stopped and then looked back up the stairs, as if some sixth sense had warned her of impending danger.

A hollow booming sound vibrated down the tunnel, the echo drumming in their ears, a terrible realization creeping over them all.

'What was that?' gasped Emily. But she knew. They all knew. Someone had slid back the rock and, like the Excisemen, they were trapped.

For a short while no one dared to put the awful truth into words and they stared at each other in silence.

'Someone closed the door,' whispered Ben at last.

'They came back,' Emily half sobbed. 'Parks and Tomson.'

Kate shuddered, imagining instead that the smugglers had risen from the dead and had imprisoned them in this terrible place.

'Maybe we can move the rock from inside,' said Ben and began to run back up the stairs. Then he let out a smothered cry and would have fallen if Emily and Kate hadn't grabbed him.

'Those bats,' he muttered as another flew over their heads. 'They're down here too.'

Emily focused her torch on the ceiling. The beam was weaker now, and with a sickening jolt they all realized that the batteries were going.

They stumbled up the steps, Emily still sweeping the tunnel with the fading beam. Then she yelled, 'Stop! Look at this.'

In the faint light they could see a small hole in the rock above them.

'It's another chimney,' said Ben desperately. 'Maybe it's a way out.'

'Most of them are blocked.' Emily was despondent.

Kate gazed up calculatingly, trying to keep calm. 'We might have to risk it.'

'If we can't push back the rock we will,' said Ben. 'That's for sure.'

They continued to climb up the steps until they arrived back at the rock that now looked depressingly solid.

Kate, Ben and Emily ran their hands over the rough surface, pushing and shoving, pulling and wrenching, but producing no results whatever.

'The door can only be opened from the other side,' said Ben eventually. 'That was the whole point – to make the Excisemen think they'd discovered a secret hide-out when it was a trap all the time. I wonder how many revenue men died of starvation on these steps – or tried to swim out and were drowned?'

As Ben talked, they were all still wrestling with the unyielding wall of rock. They knew it wasn't going to move, but they still carried on pushing and shoving until their fingers were stiff and sore.

'Surely this system of tunnels and caves *must* have been explored and mapped out?' said Kate.

Emily was born and bred in Tremaron. Could she know something that she had forgotten? 'Excisemen couldn't go on disappearing for ever!' she said desperately, hoping she might trigger Emily's memory. Deep down, however, Kate was sure that she might just as well bash her head against the rock.

'There was always something about this network that the fishing families kept secret. My mother told me never to go into the Shadow Caves, that they were evil. I never did—' Emily's voice caught on a sob, 'until I went with Roy. But we never came into this section.' Then she had another thought. 'Do you suppose Roy got trapped too? That he tried to swim out?'

'No,' said Ben abruptly. 'That's one thing you can be sure of. I'm certain he knows this system as well as the other fishermen.'

'So why wasn't Gerry Parks in on the act?' asked Kate. 'Why doesn't he know the mystery of the Shadow Caves?'

'He left Tremaron when he was in his teens,' said Emily. 'I'm sure you only get to know the secret when you start to work on the boats or marry a fisherman. It's a tradition.'

'Some tradition.' Kate was dismissive. 'This is a lethal trap. Someone should reveal the secret before it's too late.'

Too late. The words rang in their minds. Were they all going to die in the Shadow Caves?

· 9 ·

'We *are* going to get out of here alive,' promised
Kate. 'I *know* we are.' But her voice was weak in
the dank half-light.

'Let's get back to that chimney,' suggested
Ben, more optimistically than he felt. 'If it *is* a
chimney.'

'It's our only chance, so we'd better give it a go,'
said Emily miserably. All her hopes of finding
Roy had disappeared now. 'It's my fault,' she
muttered. 'Persuading you to come with me.'

'You didn't force us,' said Kate, moved by her obvious distress. 'We came of our own free will.'

Emily focused the ever weakening torch beam up at the dark space above.

'We'll have to give it a try,' said Ben, trying to be reassuring. 'Suppose the tide covers these steps.'

They stood in silence, listening to the sound of the water lapping even closer now. Emily shone her torch down the steps but they could see nothing.

'We mustn't waste the batteries any more than we have to,' said Kate. 'Besides, I don't think I *want* to know where the tide is.'

Grabbing at a projecting rock in the sloping wall, Ben pulled himself up, got a foothold and sprang – and then tumbled down again, bruising himself on the rocky floor.

On the second attempt he was successful, clinging to the rock, bracing himself and then risking another foothold which miraculously held. Then he braced himself again, reached up and swung himself into the chimney.

'It's not too bad,' he said encouragingly.

'We're not as tall as you are,' muttered Kate.

She was more agile, however, and soon reached her brother as he inched his way up the chimney, leaning back against the rock and trying to find footholds.

Emily, however, had much more difficulty, continually slipping back to lie in a crumpled heap on the steps, and on one attempt even bouncing painfully down them.

'Try again,' yelled Kate. 'Really go for it!'

Eventually Emily managed to wedge herself in, and they began to make slow, shaky progress, the shaft narrowing slightly, enabling them to get a slightly better grip with their hands and feet.

The climb seemed endless and the torch was increasingly useless as the chimney twisted in a never-ending spiral.

Ben was continually haunted by the likely possibility they would come to a dead end and Kate was already wondering what they would do if they had to come all the way down again, only to find the steps under water.

Resolutely, they forced themselves to concentrate on the climb, not wanting to think ahead as they pulled themselves on, bracing their backs against the wall of the chimney, their breath coming in short, sharp gasps, their hands slippery with sweat.

Suddenly, Ben gave a great whoop of joy. 'I can see daylight,' he yelled, and glorious relief surged in them all.

Slowly the pale glow became brighter and the shaft straightened; it was narrower now, but their painful progress became faster, the bracing easier, the niches more plentiful.

Kate and Emily felt elated, the joy spreading inside them, while Ben wanted to shout with happiness. Instead, he saved his strength and continued to climb.

'Just another few metres,' he gasped, 'and we've done it.'

As he hauled himself over the lip of the chimney, Ben's relief abruptly disappeared.

'What can you see?' called Kate.

'Not a lot.'

'What do you mean?' She dragged herself out and saw for herself.

They were on a broad ledge above the sea. Below them was a sheer drop, the waves rolling in and out of the caves.

'There's no way down,' said Ben in despair, gazing at the incoming tide beating at the rocks.

'Or up,' added Kate, gazing at the sheer cliff face in disbelief. They were just as trapped as they had ever been. Had the Excisemen been lured up here too? Would they soon see their bleached bones?

The spray rose from the caves below as the

tide filled every opening and every tunnel. The wind was mounting now, screaming about their ears, whistling around the rocks, beating at them so relentlessly that, for a moment, Kate thought she was going to be blown over the edge into the abyss.

'When they finally realize we're missing, they'll have to send a helicopter,' said Ben hopefully.

'They won't even *start* searching for a long time.' Emily was despondent. 'We'd better find somewhere to stick it out until the weather improves. They'll never reach us in these conditions.'

'There's no cover,' said Kate bleakly. 'No cover at all.'

'We could always go down again.' Ben gazed up in dismay at the large, swollen thunder clouds.

Despite their predicament none of them wanted to take that option unless they were forced to.

Then Emily heard, or thought she heard, a scrabbling sound, although it was almost impossible to tell with the wind screeching so loudly. 'I think there's someone coming up the chimney,' she whispered.

'Rubbish!' said Ben uncertainly. 'Unless it's a particularly large bat,' he ended sarcastically.

'I can hear something too,' said Kate. 'I'm sure I can.'

Ben listened carefully, and at last heard what he thought was heavy breathing. 'It's Parks,' he muttered, picking up a large chunk of rock.

'You can't hit him with that,' protested Kate.

'I can threaten him, though.' Ben walked slowly across to the chimney and peered down. Then he gave a strangled cry of surprise. 'I don't believe it.'

'Believe what?' yelled Kate as she and Emily dashed to the edge.

'Is that you, Roy?' shouted Emily hopefully.

'No,' said an angry voice. 'It's the ghost of an Exciseman.'

Alex Banner was slowly but surely clambering up towards them.

They all felt enormous relief as he emerged. If Alex was here, he must know the way out.

But all he could say as he dragged himself on to the ledge above was, 'You idiots! You complete, raving, stupid idiots!'

'Thanks a lot,' said Ben. 'We nearly got killed. You could have warned us about these caves, couldn't you? Then we wouldn't have fallen into the trap.'

'Everyone knows the Shadow Caves are dangerous. You shouldn't have come here at all.'

Alex was gazing furiously at Emily. '*You* know how dangerous the network is. Why didn't you tell them?'

'I wanted to find Roy,' she muttered.

'You're an even bigger idiot than they are.'

'OK.' Emily was prepared to come clean. 'I admit I was stupid. I wasn't thinking straight.' Then she gave Alex a withering look. 'The trouble is, some of us never really know what's going on in Tremaron. It's about time you fishermen got your act together. You and your stupid little secret. That trap's deadly.'

'Why *didn't* you help us, Alex?' Kate was equally hostile. 'Instead of copping out like that.'

'I came, didn't I?'

'A bit late, weren't you?' she snapped.

'I've always known about the trap,' said Alex, with maddening superiority. 'As Emily says, most fishermen in Tremaron do.' He shot her a scornful glance. 'I opened the rock, just like you did. Then I closed it again, in case Parks and Tomson were around.' He paused. 'Of course I knew about the escape route.'

'*Who* closed that rock on us.' Kate was livid. 'Was it you? If so—'

'No,' said Alex indignantly. 'It wasn't.'

'So how are we going to get back?' asked Kate,

calming down a little. 'It's not much fun here – in case you hadn't noticed.'

Alex gazed around him uncertainly. 'Where is it?'

'Where's what?' said Ben shortly.

'There was an iron ladder up to the next ledge,' he said. 'It was here only a few weeks ago.'

'Do you mean *this*?' asked Emily, walking over to a rusty stain on the rock which still had a couple of corroded rungs embedded in it. 'Looks as if it's finally collapsed, doesn't it? Got washed away by the weather.' She sounded absurdly triumphant, delighted that Alex had lost face, ignoring the fact that they were all trapped together on the ledge.

'That's going to create quite a problem.' Alex frowned up at the sheer rock face, his eyes searching for footholds and finding none.

Kate could almost feel the fear in him and saw the little drops of sweat on his forehead.

'How did you know we were here?' demanded Ben. He still felt confident that Alex would find a way out.

'Gerry Parks was down at the harbour talking to Sam Tomson. He looked spooked out of his mind and Tomson was telling him that he was a fool to believe in the shadow ghosts. Then Parks said he'd heard footsteps and talking in the caves. I checked at Marlow House and your mum told me you'd gone out so it didn't take long to realize how stupid you'd been. Fancy letting Emily lead you on like that.' Alex was still searching the cliff face for some kind of grip.

'Is Roy here?' asked Ben, refusing to get riled.

'I hope so,' said Alex, his eyes still desperately scanning the cliff. 'Maybe he can get us out of this mess.'

'What do Parks and Tomson want him for?' asked Emily. 'He's my uncle and I've a right to know. I came out here to make sure he was safe. Try to get him to face it out. I know he didn't take that money.'

'You *do* know he's here, don't you, Alex?' said Kate.

He nodded reluctantly. 'I just hope he's in a position to help us, that's all.'

'The position,' yelled out a voice above them, 'is a bit on the dodgy side.'

'Roy?' shouted Emily. 'Is that really you?'

'It's not Long John Silver. Now grab this.' A rope came snaking down with a harness at the end of it. 'Which of you is the lightest?'

'Is there a ledge up there?' asked Kate, peering up to see a small wiry man with a bushy beard and moustache.

'I'm not standing on thin air.'

Ben felt a surge of red-hot fury. 'I've got a question,' he shouted.

'Can't it wait? I can hardly hear you as it is. Haven't you noticed there's a storm building up?'

'Was it you who closed the trap?' Ben was shaking with anger.

'I had to.'

Kate was outraged. 'Do you know what we've been through?' she yelled.

'I would have rescued you.' They could only just make out his reply through the howling of the mounting gale. 'Now whoever's the lightest get in that harness fast.'

· 10 ·

As Roy Pearson slowly hauled Kate up towards the ledge, she swung out over the surf that rose above the reef in a murky haze. As it lashed the shore, she wondered if the slender harness was going to hold. But it did. The others followed.

As the heaviest, Ben was the last to go, and as he went he knew the sea below him was waiting, the cold, hostile waves ready to suck him down. If Roy made the slightest mistake he would be finished.

In a few more seconds, however, Ben was safely up, feeling sick and light-headed.

'You OK?' asked Roy.

'I might be sick,' Ben replied in a wobbling voice.

'Try not to. The wind's against us.' Roy detached the rope from the harness. 'Come with me. I don't want to hang around out here and advertise myself.'

They followed him through a narrow slit in the rock. Once inside, they were in semi-darkness and Kate gasped as she gazed up at the ceiling.

'Don't disturb my furry friends.' Roy spoke slowly, regretfully. 'They've been good company.'

'Why didn't you make sure you'd trapped the right people?' asked Ben, still incredibly angry at what Roy had done.

'I almost got Parks but he did a runner,' he explained hastily. 'He was screaming fit to bust so he must have seen the shadows. They're only a trick of the light.'

'Perhaps he saw the other trick – your plastic skeleton,' observed Ben drily.

'So why close the trap?' In the back of her mind Kate realized that this argument wasn't going to get them anywhere, but her relief and fury were so great she couldn't stop herself.

'I pushed the rock back in position because I thought Sam Tomson might persuade Gerry to come back into the caves at any moment. Anyway, I didn't want to blow the secret. It's Tremaron's own. Now why don't you postpone all this until I've got you out of here?'

'Do you really promise you were going to rescue us?' Kate was trembling with delayed shock.

'Of course I promise,' shouted Roy Pearson. 'Do you think I'd let you all die – like the Excisemen? What sort of person do you think I am?' He hurried on quickly. 'I'm sorry about what's happened and the danger I've put you all in,' Roy finished rather lamely. 'I should have faced it out,' he added, 'but I'd got so worried I wasn't thinking straight. The truth is I couldn't keep up with the repayments on those new video games in the arcade and the people I borrowed from were getting heavy, so I decided to magic myself away for a bit.' No one laughed and Roy turned to Emily. 'I was afraid Parks and Tomson might turn up and put pressure on you, so that's why I didn't say anything.'

'Who *are* Parks and Tomson?' asked Ben curiously.

'Money lenders. Crooked money lenders,' said Roy. 'I was a fool to try and do business with them but Gerry Parks was someone I used to know. We were friends when we were kids and we got into a bit of trouble with the police. He thinks I grassed him up, but I didn't – it was his brother. But he never realized that.' Roy paused. 'Ever since then he's had this grudge against me because he got put in a detention centre – and I didn't.' He paused again and gazed up at the rock, as if he was already in some kind of prison. 'Now they're pressing me to pay up and the boys on the boats are trying to raise the money. They're *real* friends. But there's something else – extra penalty interest to be paid too. As usual I didn't read the small print in the contract, but I've had plenty of time to study it now. They're totally over the top. In fact, they've taken me to the cleaners, and however much the boys raise I could still lose the business. All I've got left is the lease.'

'Can't you get a lawyer?' asked Ben.

'And lose even more money?' Roy looked at him suspiciously. 'I don't hold with lawyers.'

Emily was certainly right about him not being much of a business man, thought Kate.

'Parks and Tomson call it keeping their books

straight,' he continued bitterly. 'It's really demanding money with menaces so that's why I'm in hiding up here. The boys will fire a maroon flare signal from one of the trawlers when they've raised what they can.' Roy paused. 'This cave is the old smugglers' hideaway,' he said, going over to the back wall where another narrow slit led into the darkness beyond. 'Once you know the network, you can be master of the Shadow Caves. I reckon I've inherited the title now.'

'I just want to know—' began Emily, but her question was interrupted by a high-pitched engine whine that penetrated the still mounting wind.

Peering cautiously from the ledge, Kate could see the motor boat careering over the waves, circling the base of the cliff.

'They must have seen me,' said Roy gloomily.

'Our fault again,' replied Kate. Now it was her turn to feel guilty.

'No,' said Alex, relenting at last. 'I should have come clean. I should have trusted you more, let you into the secret. It's hard to accept strangers in Tremaron, but I reckon you aren't strangers any longer.'

They gazed down again at the luxury motor

boat, bumping through the waves, and saw that Gerry Parks had focused his binoculars on the cliff face.

'That's the *Sea Queen*. She belongs to Sam Tomson,' explained Roy. 'The kind of craft he *would* have. She's usually moored in the marina up the coast. He's a fool to bring her out in this weather.'

'Why don't you just sit tight?' suggested Kate. 'They might have seen you but they'll never reach you.'

'I've got to see you lot safely home,' said Roy despondently. 'It's my fault you're here at all.'

'You can't give yourself up because of us,' Ben insisted. 'We'll hang on until the fishermen raise the money.' He glanced across at Kate. He knew she was thinking about Mum and Dad who would be worried out of their minds by now.

'What beats me is why Parks should have started searching in the caves at all,' Roy was saying. 'I chose them as a hiding place because I thought it was the last place they'd look.'

'I think I can explain that,' said Kate, and told them all about Tracy-Anne.

Alex was furious but Roy only looked miserable. 'She used to be a friend,' he said wistfully.

90

'Wait.' Ben was staring out across the tumultuous sea towards the harbour. 'Wasn't that a flare going up? It's difficult to see in all this spray.'

'There's another one,' yelled Emily. 'They've got the money!'

'At least I can pay them something,' said Roy. He sounded more anxious than pleased, as if all this hiding out had still been in vain.

'What about that extra interest?' asked Emily uneasily.

'I'll sort it out.' He shrugged. 'Maybe I'll have to do another runner. But this time further away.'

'You can't do that,' Alex urged him. 'You've got to stay and face it out now.'

Roy strode towards the slit at the back of the cave as if he couldn't bear to hear any more. 'As the tide's still in we're going for another climb.' He gazed up at the bats for a moment and his voice shook as he said, 'I appreciate everyone's help.'

'We're all behind you,' said Alex determinedly. 'Don't go and do anything stupid now.'

Kate, however, was wondering if she was the only one who had noticed the cash box half concealed under a tarpaulin. She glanced at Ben but he, like the others, was already following Roy through the narrow slit in the rock.

Kate realized she might just have time to try and check out the box. Could Roy really have taken the money from the arcade? Was he planning to make off with the cash once the fishermen had paid off at least some of his debts? Was he playing one off against the other?

As Alex struggled through the narrow gap Kate darted over to the tarpaulin, pulled it aside and picked up the box. It was heavy.

She rattled it but there was no sound. Perhaps it was stuffed with bank notes? How long was it since Roy had been to the bank?

'What are you doing?' whispered Ben, making her jump so badly that Kate's heart thumped painfully. 'I came back for you.'

'I found this.'

'A cash box.'

'And it's heavy,' said Kate.

'You mean it's Roy's?' Ben seemed to be very unwilling to latch on to what she was saying.

'Come on!' Roy Pearson's voice echoed from the crevice. 'What's the hold up?'

Kate shoved the cash box back under the tarpaulin. 'We're coming,' she yelled. 'I thought I'd dropped something.' Had she aroused his suspicions, she wondered. Her excuse certainly sounded feeble.

'What are we going to do?' hissed Ben.

'We'll sort it out later,' Kate whispered as they ran to the narrow slit in the rock.

'There's a chimney.' Roy was brusque. 'It's not difficult.'

As he braced himself against the rock wall, gazing up yet another dark and uninviting shaft at the thunder clouds, Ben wondered over and over again if Roy Pearson was conning them all. Was that cash box loaded with money, carefully packed for a getaway?

Kate was thinking much the same as she pushed and pulled her way up the chimney.

Eventually, they dragged themselves over the edge on to the short, wind-blown grass of the cliff top that was the springiest turf imaginable after they had been underground for so long.

Kate felt like hugging the earth or jumping up and down in the gale, just to remind herself of the miraculous escape they had had.

'Where are we going?' asked Alex. 'Back to Tremaron?'

Roy was gazing down at the sea, his long black hair flying in the wind. 'The *Sea Queen*'s in trouble,' he said. 'They're on a lee shore and it looks as if their engine's packed up.'

The motor boat was drifting sideways towards the wave-lashed rocks.

Alex watched with increasing alarm. 'They haven't a clue. No wonder they spent so much time in the marina.'

Ben watched Sam Tomson trying to drop anchor and Gerry Parks staggering to the bows of the speedboat with an inflatable in his arms.

'They're going to hit the rocks,' said Roy. 'They don't stand a chance.'

Seconds later a huge wave flipped the *Sea Queen* over and for a moment neither of her occupants could be seen in the boiling surf. Then Ben spotted them, floundering in the waves.

'They'll drown,' yelled Kate.

Roy was already running down the cliff path and the others followed, slipping and sliding on the wet clay, just keeping their feet, the wind battering at them.

Finally they arrived on the beach, only to see mountainous wave crests but no sign at all of Gerry Parks or Sam Tomson.

'There they are,' yelled Ben.

The two men suddenly surfaced, the lashing wind driving them between the rocks towards a patch of sand.

'Wait for the next wave to pull back,' shouted

Roy. 'And then try and drag them in.'

All Kate could hear was the roaring of the surf. Although Parks and Tomson had miraculously survived so far, she knew it would be difficult to bring them to safety; the undertow was incredibly strong.

'Go!' yelled Roy, and he, Alex and Kate sprinted towards Gerry Parks while Emily and Ben went for Sam Tomson as the wave rolled back.

'Get up,' yelled Ben.

Somehow Tomson staggered to his feet, and they dragged both men across the wet sand, chased by the next wave as it clutched at their knees, trying to suck them out again.

'You're lucky,' gasped Roy Pearson. 'Amazingly lucky.'

As Gerry Parks and Sam Tomson lay on the beach, shaking and shivering, Alex said, 'Who's that up there on the cliff top?'

'It's Tracy-Anne,' said Emily in surprise. 'She's ducked down again now.'

Ben wondered once again if they were in it together, that the enmity between Roy and Tracy-Anne had been simply a front. Somehow he must talk to the others alone. He glanced at

Emily and Alex doubtfully. They weren't going to like what he and Kate had to tell them.

'You've been avoiding your creditors,' Parks was wheezing ungratefully.

Beside him, Tomson struggled to speak but failed.

'We could have left you out there to drown,' Alex shouted.

'You kids,' gasped Sam Tomson. 'You've been protecting him.'

'I can pay you back,' said Roy. 'The money's being put in your account this afternoon.' He paused and then obviously decided to bluff it out. 'But not the penalty interest.'

'It's got to be paid. It's in the contract.'

'My lawyers will be dealing with that,' said Roy with sudden and surprising authority. 'You must realize that if you press any claim all payments will probably be frozen until after the court hearing – and that's going to take some time.'

He's become so much more confident, thought Ben. Was Roy Pearson working to a deliberately laid plan? He gazed up to the cliff top but there was no sign of Tracy-Anne.

Parks and Tomson exchanged glances.

'All right,' spluttered Tomson. 'I'm prepared to waive the penalty interest providing—' He paused, still gasping for breath. 'Providing all back payments are made instantly and future sums are received on time.' He ended on a fit of coughing.

'They will be,' said Roy.

Parks and Tomson dragged themselves slowly to their feet, shivering but saying nothing.

'Better get moving,' said Roy with a grin. 'It's a long way to Tremaron from here.'

'What about air-sea rescue?' demanded Tomson.

'You've *been* rescued,' said Roy. 'Now get going.'

'Let's make it a jog,' suggested Emily maliciously. 'You'll soon dry off.'

Groaning, Gerry Parks and Sam Tomson burst into a lumbering stumbling, choking run.

Kate and Ben gazed at the Shadow Caves as the water music grew louder.

'The tide's on the ebb,' she said.

The sound was as chilling as ever and Ben shuddered. He never wanted to go back into the caves ever again.

Alex came up behind them.

'Come home with us, Alex,' Ben said. 'There's something we've got to tell you.'

Alex gazed at him warily. 'More surprises?' he asked.

'Surprises maybe,' Ben replied. 'But not enough evidence to back them up.'

'We'll talk later,' said Roy when they had reached Tremaron. I'm going to take Emily home now.'

'OK.' Kate paused at the front door of Marlow House. 'I do hope Mum's not on the war-path.'

They walked nervously into reception, only to find their mother comforting the soaked figures of Sam Tomson and Gerry Parks.

'What a dreadful business,' she was saying. 'And how awful to lose your boat. Can I suggest a couple of brandies on the house?'

'Well,' said Sam Tomson, 'that wouldn't go amiss.'

Mrs Lewis whipped round as Kate, Ben and Alex tried to sneak past her, making for the stairs.

'Where have you lot been? You're absolutely filthy.'

'Didn't they tell you, Mum?' asked Kate, gazing innocently at the blue, teeth-chattering faces of Parks and Tomson.

'Tell me what?' she asked indignantly.

'We rescued Mr Tomson and Mr Parks. They owe us their lives,' said Ben grandly.

'Is this true?' Mum wheeled back to the shivering pair.

Sam Tomson muttered something none of them could hear.

· 11 ·

Sitting on the spare room bed, Alex listened carefully to what they had to say without a flicker of expression on his face. When they had finished, he spoke with conviction. 'Roy would never do a terrible thing like that.'

'I knew you'd say that,' said Kate bitterly. 'If you're a fisherman you can't do any wrong.'

'He's not a fisherman,' replied Alex.

'Maybe not. But Roy's part of the community, isn't he? You just look after your own.' She shoved a pot of pencils across the desk so roughly that some of them fell out. Replacing them quickly, Kate took out her case book.

'He wouldn't let the fishermen pay off his debts and then just push off with a load of cash,' Alex insisted.

'Tracy-Anne was up on the cliffs, near where we came out of that chimney. Suppose she went there to meet Roy and they had some kind of thing going together.' Ben was determined to jerk Alex out of his complacency.

He was, however, completely unruffled. 'They might have gone out together for a while, but they can't stand each other now.'

'That could be just what they want people to think.'

'They've made a pretty good job of it then.' He was completely calm and not in the least shaken by the others' suspicions. 'If anyone pinched the takings you can bet your life it was Tracy-Anne herself. She's going around with Mark Dowling now—'

'Another fisherman?' asked Kate.

Alex grinned with sudden warmth. 'No. He's a drop out from London. But Dowling's got plans.'

'What plans?'

'Wants to set himself up in the motor trade in Padstow and could do with a little capital.

However small.' He paused thoughtfully. 'Now you mention it, they've both been seen chatting to Parks and Tomson.'

'You mean they could finance them?' asked Ben slowly.

'Well, if Roy went down – lost everyone's respect and was allowed to go bankrupt – they could repossess the machines, maybe even get their hands on the arcade *and* give Dowling a bit on the side as a reward if he and Tracy-Anne have helped to blacken Roy's name. Maybe they've always had their eye on the business.' Alex paused. 'Parks and Tomson are the last kind of people we want moving in on Tremaron.'

'We haven't got any evidence,' said Kate grudgingly.

Alex frowned. 'We could get some.'

'How?'

'Watch her caravan.'

'That could take too long,' said Ben.

Alex was silent, racking his brains. 'There's always Mrs Cosham.'

She lived at the top of the town, next door to the Methodist chapel. As the three of them walked up the narrow streets, Emily suddenly emerged from one of the alleys.

'Where have you lot been?' she demanded.

'Having a meeting,' said Kate.

'So you were leaving me out?' Emily was annoyed. 'After all I did.'

'After you nearly killed us,' said Kate in a measured voice. Then she relented. 'We're going to see Mrs Cosham.'

'What for?'

'To see if she can shop Tracy-Anne,' said Alex hopefully.

Mrs Cosham was scrubbing the steps of the chapel when they arrived, but she didn't look at all pleased to see them.

'What do you lot want?' she asked, still kneeling and scrubbing.

'We found Roy,' said Kate.

She stood up slowly. 'Where?'

'In the caves. He was waiting for the fishermen to raise some money so he could pay Parks and Tomson for those machines.'

'And have they?'

'Yes,' said Alex. 'There's some penalty interest left but Roy threatened them with a lawyer and they decided not to collect it.'

'They will,' she said gloomily. 'They're a pair of crooks. I used to know Gerry Parks when he was a kid. Right little con man. He used to sell anything he could get his hands on. I remember he tried to sell me the lady next door's dustbin once, when mine was swept away in the floods.'

'Did you know a lot of money went missing from the arcade?' asked Emily hesitantly.

Mrs Cosham nodded grimly. 'I heard.'

'We're sure Roy didn't take it,' said Alex solidly. 'But the question is – who did? If we don't find out and everyone believes he's just on the make, the fishermen might decide not to back Roy after all and then Parks and Tomson could bankrupt him, maybe get their hands on the lease for the arcade and the shop.'

Mrs Cosham went white with anger. 'They'd better not try.'

'Do you know who took the money?' asked Alex bluntly.

'I like Roy,' she said slowly, not answering directly, 'but he was desperate – maybe the whole thing got on top of him and he just wanted to cut and run.'

They stared at Mrs Cosham, horrified that she thought Roy was capable of such a thing.

'What about Tracy-Anne?' asked Emily fiercely. 'She's much more likely to have taken it, isn't she?'

Mrs Cosham's lip curled in contempt. 'She wouldn't have the wit.' She paused. 'Would she?'

'She might,' said Emily encouragingly. 'She just might.'

Kate and Ben kept thinking about the cash box in the cave. They also knew Emily and Alex were trying *not* to think about it.

'What we need to do,' said Emily, 'is to scare Tracy-Anne into giving herself away.' She gazed enquiringly at Mrs Cosham. 'Got any ideas?'

'I might have.' She appeared to be thinking hard. Then a broad smile spread over her narrow face. 'Suppose I tell Tracy-Anne I heard this rumour that the police are searching the homes of all Roy's employees?'

'Shouldn't take long,' muttered Alex. 'There's only two of you.'

Mrs Cosham wasn't in the least deterred. 'Where's Roy now?'

Emily shrugged. 'He came in to have some tea – and went out again.'

Where, wondered Ben with a nasty lurch in the pit of his stomach. Did he return to the Shadow Caves to pick up the money? Was he going to make a rendezvous with Tracy-Anne? They all four exchanged uneasy glances.

'I'll take a risk,' said Mrs Cosham at last. 'She might give herself away.'

As Mrs Cosham hurried back inside her cottage, Ben headed up the plan of campaign.

'If Tracy-Anne's got the money she'll take it out of the caravan and try to hide it.'

106

'And we'll follow her,' suggested Alex. 'See what she does with it.'

'If it's there,' warned Kate. If only she had had the time to open that cash box. Then she realized it would probably have been locked anyway.

'We can't go after her in a pack,' said Emily. 'We'll hide near the caravan in pairs. Me and Alex. You and Kate.'

The locals versus the newcomers, thought Ben sadly. He remembered Alex saying how he accepted them now but would they ever *really* belong to Tremaron?

Mrs Cosham returned with a broad smile. 'She's got her knickers in a twist. Slammed down the phone she did.'

· 12 ·

It was getting dark as the four of them crept towards the caravan, watching out for the caretaker. Kate had been worrying that Tracy-Anne might have already left, but now she could see lights in the windows and could hear voices.

'There's plenty of cover in the long grass,' whispered Emily. 'Alex and I'll go this side – you two the other.'

Alex shook his head. 'No. I'll go with Kate and you go with Ben.'

Kate gave him a friendly grin and Ben felt better. Maybe they were real insiders now.

Crouching down, they waited for such a long time that they began to wonder if Tracy-Anne had decided to stay in her caravan and sit it out.

Darkness began to spread over the headland and a nightjar's song repeated itself relentlessly until it began to get on their already over-stretched nerves.

Then, suddenly, the door of the caravan opened and Tracy-Anne hurried out, carrying a bag. She looked round furtively, and as she began to walk up the road towards the cliffs, the door opened again and a man stood on the steps of the caravan, waving his fist.

'Good riddance,' he yelled. 'And don't come back.'

'I wouldn't dream of it,' bellowed Tracy-Anne. 'Thank heavens I never married you. It would be like living with a tramp.'

'He won't do you any better,' snarled Dowling.

'He couldn't do me any worse. At least he's a man, not a mouse,' she yelled as the door of the caravan slammed and Tracy-Anne stumbled on her way.

Why was she going up the cliff? The path led back to the top of the Shadow Caves, and Roy's escape route. Were they going to hide in the tunnels together, wondered Ben. Did Tracy-Anne have the stolen money in her bag, or was that already in the cash box?

Following Tracy-Anne over the cliff top was a difficult task although the wind had died down and the long-awaited storm had passed over without breaking. The four of them strung out in a line, ducking down, using every possible piece of scanty cover.

Tracy-Anne, however, never looked back, striding on, her energy fuelled by anger or fear or a combination of both.

Why on earth was she climbing up a cliff with a bag, Alex wondered. He now realized she wasn't going towards Roy's escape chimney but continuing along the path.

In fact she was heading straight for an outcrop of rock.

'Where's she off to?' whispered Kate.

'She's making for the Devil's Chair,' said Alex. 'Maybe she wants to hand something over.'

They ducked down behind some windblown bushes, seeing that Ben and Emily had already found cover.

'She *has* to be meeting someone,' Kate whispered. 'She can't just be going to admire the view.'

Slowly, cautiously, they started to follow Tracy-Anne again as she reached the headland and the rocks that only vaguely resembled a chair.

'Tracy-Anne.' The voice was all too familiar and they gazed at each other in dismay.

Roy Pearson had emerged from behind the Devil's Chair and he was carrying the cash box Kate had discovered in the Shadow Caves.

'What do you want?' Tracy-Anne spat out viciously.

'I want to see what you've got in that bag.'

'It's none of your business.'

'You've got the arcade money, haven't you?'

'Rubbish!' she shrilled.

'Then why are you climbing up to the Devil's Chair on a dark night like this?'

'She's come to stitch you up, Pearson.' Two men rose from the other side of the rocks and in the milky-white moonlight Ben could see they were Gerry Parks and Sam Tomson.

'How?' asked Roy. He looked completely thrown.

Sam Tomson moved threateningly towards him. 'It's quite simple. Tracy-Anne has the money in her bag. We're going to hand it back to you.'

'That's good of you. It's my money, after all.'

'The cash you stole from your own business so you could do a runner from Tremaron at last,' said Tomson with a sneer.

'Now why should I want to do that?' asked Roy mildly. 'Last time I went to London I got so homesick I had to come back.'

'You weren't bankrupt then,' said Parks. 'We'll see to it that you are now.'

'The money's been transferred to your account—'

'Not the interest though,' smiled Tomson. 'The fishermen won't be so keen to help you out any more when you're found up here with all that money stuffed in your pockets.' He paused. 'The situation will be quite clear to everyone. You hid the money, let the fishermen pay off your debts, and then went back to collect the cash before you took off.'

Gerry Parks took over. 'When you've gone – and you know you can't stay – we'll repossess the machines and take over the arcade. With a bit of professionalism, that place could be a nice little earner.' He frowned. 'Local boy comes home to make good. I always liked Tremaron, and I deserve a second chance. My turn to have a break, eh, Roy?'

There was a long silence.

'Hold it,' said Alex, clambering out from the

cover of some bushes.

Emily, Kate and Ben also stood up, nervous but relieved that Roy Pearson was in the clear.

'We're witnesses,' explained Kate. 'We heard every word of what you said.' She turned to Roy. 'What *is* in that cash box then?'

'All my account books and the lease for the arcade,' he replied. 'And the so-called contract I had with these two. Do you want to see them?'

She shook her head.

'No one's going to believe a pack of kids—' began Gerry Parks, but his voice lacked conviction.

'Give me the bag, Tracy-Anne,' said Roy quietly.

'No way.'

'What were you doing on the cliffs while we were rescuing these two?' demanded Ben.

Tracy-Anne shrugged. 'Believe it or not I was worried about the *Sea Queen*. The weather was bad, I knew they weren't experienced enough to—'

Without pausing to think, Ben grabbed Tracy-Anne round the waist. She fell over with a scream and Alex picked up the bag.

'Give me that bag,' yelled Tracy-Anne, picking herself up from the ground and giving Ben a murderous glance. 'It contains my personal belongings.'

Alex bent down and snapped open the clasp. Inside was clothing and a washbag and a large brown parcel that was torn at one edge. In the moonlight he could see wads of five pound notes. 'You seem to have got Roy's money here too,' he said with a grin.

'Hand it over.' Sam Tomson began to walk purposefully towards Alex.

'Quick, all of you,' shouted Roy. 'We'll get back down that chimney.'

They all four followed him as he ran back towards the entrance to the caves, while Parks and Tomson dragged Tracy-Anne to her feet.

'Get after them!' she shrieked. 'Get that money back.'

Dragging out a torch from his pocket, Roy plunged down into the darkness, trying to provide enough light for Alex, Kate, Emily and Ben to see what they were doing. The single beam wasn't very adequate, but somehow they managed to find hand- and footholds, slipping and sliding but just avoiding losing their grip. Alex, still clinging on to Tracy-Anne's bag, had the hardest job of all.

'Where are we going?' he gasped. 'Back to the smugglers' trap?'

'I've got something better than that.' Roy sounded triumphant. 'They won't get out of it in a hurry either.'

Suddenly there was a spluttering, groaning sound and they knew Parks and Tomson were also trying to scramble down the chimney. Then they heard a familiar voice yell, 'I'm ruining my shoes.'

'Get 'em off,' Tomson ordered, 'or you'll fall.'

'They cost a fortune,' she protested, but almost immediately Tracy-Anne's high-heeled shoes hit Emily a glancing blow as they dropped down the chimney.

Seconds later, Tracy-Anne began to scream, and Alex noticed the bats were rising towards her in a soft, downy, fluttering cloud.

'I'm going to fall!' Her voice was shrill.

As Roy flashed up the torch, they could see she was in a decidedly precarious position, clinging to a rocky outcrop with both hands, her feet scrabbling for a hold. Above her Tomson and Parks barked useless commands.

'You shouldn't have let me go down first,' she bellowed. 'You're just a couple of cowards. Someone help me. Please.'

'Twist your foot sideways,' advised Roy. 'There's a cleft in the rock.'

'Where?'

'To the right.'

Her foot overshot. Now she was dangling in space, her thin wrists stretched almost to breaking point.

'You've gone too far!' Roy yelled. 'Back a bit.'

Tracy-Anne's feet scrabbled and found the niche. But, despite the fact the pressure was no longer on her wrists, she didn't seem inclined to move.

'Get on with it,' snapped Parks. 'We can't hang around here all night.'

'I can't see,' she protested.

'There's only one torch,' replied Roy. 'And I'm shining it on your feet. All you need is instinct.'

'I don't have any,' Tracy-Anne whimpered.

'Move your left foot down.'

'No way.'

'And there's a niche for your hand. Look, you can see it in the wall. It's big and easy.'

Tracy-Anne didn't move.

'I can see it too,' said Kate, as Roy flashed the torch over the wall. 'You can do it easily,' she added, trying to be as reassuring as she could.

'I can't.' Tracy-Anne's voice was tight with fear. 'I can't move. I can't move at all.'

'You've *got* to!' Tomson was far from being sympathetic. 'You've got us trapped.'

'I'm going to fall!' Tracy-Anne began to

scream again, the sound echoing in the shaft. Then she saw the bats below her, still fluttering, probably as terrified as she was. 'What's that?'

'Bats,' replied Alex bleakly.

Tracy-Anne's screams redoubled.

'I'll have to go up there,' said Roy.

'You can't.' Ben was adamant. 'There's not enough room. I'll go.'

'You can't,' said Kate woodenly.

'I'm the nearest. I'll have to.' Ben began to climb and they all watched in silence as Roy guided him with the torch and Tracy-Anne's screams became, if possible, even louder.

'Shut up!' yelled Roy and Sam Tomson in unison.

Tracy-Anne opened her mouth wide but no sound came out.

She'll have them both down, thought Kate, as her brother swarmed up the wall.

'OK,' said Ben. 'I'll guide your feet.'

'You won't touch them,' Tracy-Anne replied, and to everyone's horror she kicked out at him.

'Stop kicking!' yelled Ben. 'You'll have us both off.' He looked down at the drop below. It was a yawning dark chasm, and he knew that if they fell they would be badly hurt. For the first time he was really afraid, his fear of heights drawing at him, trying to pull him down with a far greater force than Tracy-Anne's kicking feet. As long as he was busy it was all right, but once he stopped to think, the horrible panicky feeling had him in its grip. 'I can help you.' Ben tried to sound as full of authority as he could, but he knew his voice was shaking. Tracy-Anne's hands were gradually slipping and unless he calmed her quickly she would fall and take him with her. 'I can help you,' he repeated, 'but you've got to listen to me.'

'Yes,' said Parks threateningly. 'Listen to him. Get your act together.' Unfortunately, his impatient words only increased her panic.

'You can *see* I can't move!' she yelled.

'Let Ben do the talking,' said Roy steadily. 'If you don't, they'll both go.'

Parks and Tomson stayed quiet as Ben said cautiously, 'Tracy-Anne?'

She didn't reply.

'Tracy-Anne?'

Still she didn't reply.

'There's no need to worry. I can guide your feet into crevices. Just hang on with your hands and then work them down. Do exactly what I say.'

'OK,' she whispered.

Ben felt a soaring sense of triumph. Tracy-Anne sounded as if she might co-operate at last.

But he knew he was only at the beginning. He risked a second glance down and felt the dreadful drawing sensation again. I mustn't look down, he told himself firmly. If I do, it'll be the end of both of us. Bracing himself against the rock he eased her feet into a niche, one after the other. 'Well done. Now put your hand over there.'

Roy swept the rock with the torch beam.

'I can't.'

'You can. It's easy. Just do it.'

Clumsily, Tracy-Anne did it.

'Easy now,' said Ben, elated but knowing they still had a long way to go. 'Take it slowly.'

Gradually he began to talk her down, while Parks and Tomson above them and Roy, Kate, Alex and Emily below remained silent. It's all on me, Ben told himself over and over again. I've got to keep calm.

Slowly, with shaking hands and feet, Tracy-Anne began to descend. Then she paused. 'Where are those bats?' she demanded.

'I think you've frightened the whole bunch away.' Roy was very convincing. 'They won't come back.'

Fortunately there didn't seem to be any sign of them at all, although Kate was sure she could make out a whistling sound in the shadowed rock. She hoped against hope that Tracy-Anne hadn't heard it too.

Ben continued to give measured instructions and gradually an atmosphere of concentrated calm began to develop on the rock wall.

'That's right,' he said. 'Put your foot down here and your hand over there.'

Tracy-Anne gasped as her grip seemed to slip, but this time she quickly regained it. 'Is that OK?'

'That's fine. Just do what I say.' Ben could feel her confidence building, sense that she trusted him, but he knew he couldn't start getting complacent.

'What's that?' Tracy-Anne's voice was suddenly shrill. 'I felt something – something soft.'

'It's nothing.'

'You sure?'

'Yes.' In fact Ben knew that a solitary bat had been disturbed in the darkness, but he certainly wasn't going to tell Tracy-Anne. 'Come on – we haven't got far to go now. Left with your hand. Right with your foot. There's plenty of space for you to grip.'

There was a loud cheer from below as Tracy-Anne eventually landed on the ground, falling into Ben's arms with a loud wail.

'You make a lovely couple,' commented Alex.

As Tomson and Parks rapidly began to descend, partly helped by Roy's torch, Kate whispered, 'We still can't trust those two.'

'We're going out on to the ledge,' replied Roy. 'I've got some climbing gear here.'

Once Parks and Tomson were safely nearing the ground, Roy snapped off his torch, grabbed a rope and hurried out. The others followed him, staring down at the white crests of the waves.

'You mean we *are* going down to the trap again,' said Ben warily.

'No, we're going up,' he said. 'There's another ledge above the chimney and it's not that steep. I'll take this rope up and make it fast to a rock. Then you can join me.'

'What about the others?' asked Emily as they heard Tracy-Anne give a piercing scream.

'I think they've just met up with the bats again,' said Roy quietly as he began to climb.

Tracy-Anne was still screaming when the rope began to snake down to them.

'Let's go,' said Alex as he grabbed it, and still clutching Tracy-Anne's bag began to pull himself up. Kate, Emily and Ben followed, and when they reached the next ledge, Roy untied the rope and began to coil it in.

'They'll have to stay there until the police come if we block the top of the chimney,' he said and went over to the edge. 'Can you hear me down there?' he bellowed.

'You can't leave us,' shouted back Sam Tomson. 'Not here.'

'You'll be quite safe,' yelled Roy. 'Just don't try to go down or back up. We're going to push a rock over the chimney.'

'We'll be trapped,' screamed Gerry Parks.

'That's the idea.'

'You can't do it,' wept Tracy-Anne. 'What about these horrible bats?'

'They'll keep you company,' Roy shouted. 'They're very friendly when you get to know them.' He grinned at Ben in the moonlight. 'I'm afraid we've got to face another climb.'

'That doesn't worry us,' said Alex. 'We could scale Everest after this lot.'

'If it hadn't been for the four of you,' said Roy, 'I'd have been properly stitched up. How many more mysteries are you going to solve round here?'

'As many as Marlow House can give us,' Kate retorted.

The Mystery of
Bloodhound Island

Who is the stranger signalling
to the island?

Ben, Kate and Alex are sure the new guest
at Marlow House has booked in under a
false name. They decide to follow him to
Bloodhound Island. There, not only are
the hounds waiting for them, but the
people in the old house have a dark
secret.

The Mystery of
The White Knuckle Ride

Who is behind the ride of terror?

Sam Shepherd's fairground is being
sabotaged. The White Knuckle Ride sticks
at the top of its switchback and Ben, Kate,
Alex and Emily are among the passengers
who have to be rescued. Who are the
mystery vandals? And why are they
putting hundreds of lives at risk?

The Mystery of
Captain Keene's Treasure

Who will be first to discover
the treasure?

Captain Keene comes to stay at Marlow
House, searching for his long-lost family
fortune. He has half the treasure map but
his rival has the other half. Ben, Kate,
Alex and Emily, together with their new
friend Jamie, want to help Captain Keene,
but when the hunt moves to the
underground workings of a local tin
mine, they are all plunged into danger.